Bass Re————————————————————— ————————
guns, all of their attention on him. He grabbed for his own
gun, cleared leather smoothly, and fired.

Clint couldn't let Reeves face the three men alone this
time any more than he could have earlier that day, so he . . .
drew his gun. "Hey, Ferris!"

Only one Ferris brother even heard Clint shout, and that
was Jake. Abruptly, he turned to face Clint just as the
Gunsmith pulled the trigger twice. Both bullets struck Jake
Ferris in the chest and put him down in the street.

John and Jerry Ferris both drew on Bass Reeves, but
even if they hadn't been drunk they never would have been
fast enough . . . Reeves shot Jerry in the heart, then turned
the gun on John and did the same. In the blink of an eye
all three Ferris brothers were down on their backs, and soon
they'd be joining their brother Clem at the undertaker's.

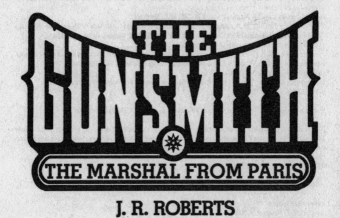

THE GUNSMITH

THE MARSHAL FROM PARIS

J. R. ROBERTS

JOVE BOOKS, NEW YORK

THE BERKLEY PUBLISHING GROUP
Published by the Penguin Group
Penguin Group (USA) Inc.
375 Hudson Street, New York, New York 10014, USA
Penguin Group (Canada), 90 Eglinton Avenue East, Suite 700, Toronto, Ontario M4P 2Y3, Canada
(a division of Pearson Penguin Canada Inc.)
Penguin Books Ltd., 80 Strand, London WC2R 0RL, England
Penguin Group Ireland, 25 St. Stephen's Green, Dublin 2, Ireland (a division of Penguin Books Ltd.)
Penguin Group (Australia), 250 Camberwell Road, Camberwell, Victoria 3124, Australia
(a division of Pearson Australia Group Pty. Ltd.)
Penguin Books India Pvt. Ltd., 11 Community Centre, Panchsheel Park, New Delhi—110 017, India
Penguin Group (NZ), 67 Apollo Drive, Rosedale, North Shore 0632, New Zealand
(a division of Pearson New Zealand Ltd.)
Penguin Books (South Africa) (Pty.) Ltd., 24 Sturdee Avenue, Rosebank, Johannesburg 2196,
South Africa

Penguin Books Ltd., Registered Offices: 80 Strand, London WC2R 0RL, England

This is a work of fiction. Names, characters, places, and incidents either are the product of the author's imagination or are used fictitiously, and any resemblance to actual persons, living or dead, business establishments, events, or locales is entirely coincidental.

THE MARSHAL FROM PARIS

A Jove Book / published by arrangement with the author

PRINTING HISTORY
Jove edition / November 2008

Copyright © 2008 by Robert J. Randisi.
Cover illustration by Sergio Giovine.

ISBN: 978-0-515-14544-1

JOVE®
Jove Books are published by The Berkley Publishing Group,
a division of Penguin Group (USA) Inc.,
375 Hudson Street, New York, New York 10014.
JOVE® is a registered trademark of Penguin Group (USA) Inc.
The "J" design is a trademark belonging to Penguin Group (USA) Inc.

PRINTED IN THE UNITED STATES OF AMERICA

10 9 8 7 6 5 4 3 2 1

ONE

Paris, Texas

Bass Reeves rode into town trailing two horses with men slung over the saddles, wrapped in blankets, dead. The badge on his chest said he was allowed to go out and hunt men and bring them back this way, as long as he had a warrant in his pocket as well. A badge and a warrant, that's all it took to kill a man and not get arrested yourself for it.

Of course Reeves, as a deputy marshal assigned to the federal district courts of Paris and Sherman, Texas, and most points south of the Red River, preferred to bring his charges back alive, so they could either serve their time out in Huntsville or be hanged for their crimes. He didn't like being executioner. That was another man's job, but sometimes men just didn't give him that luxury of bringing them back alive. Sometimes the only way they'd come back was dead.

Reeves was aware of the stares he was getting from the town folks as he rode in. The heads of the dead men were

visible and they were white. Bass Reeves was a black man—
the only black federal deputy marshal west of the Missis-
sippi.

He'd been born to slave parents, but had escaped slav-
ery after a dispute with his master over a game of cards.
Reeves had severely beaten the young man and then fled.
He ended up in Indian territory and lived for a time with
the Creek Indians until the slaves were freed. As a free-
man, he became a successful rancher and farmer, but that
wasn't the life for him. When Judge Isaac Parker was assigned to bring order to the Indian territories, Reeves was
one of two hundred men Parker deputized. Parker had
pinned a badge on Reeves because he spoke the language
of the Indian and did not suffer the red man's hatred and
inherent distrust of the white man.

He'd been wearing a badge now for over ten years, and
these days it was Texas he was cleaning up, not the Indian
territories. Reeves had become devoted to upholding the
law and was probably the most honest lawman in the West.

But he was still a black man, and there were still times
he wished he lived among the red man instead of the
white man.

This was one of those times.

White men and women lined the streets and stared at
him with hatred in their eyes. He ignored them. If any of
them wanted his attention, they'd have to step out into the
street to get it, and then they had better be prepared for it.
Reeves still carried the hundred and ninety pounds he'd
been sporting for years and although he was in his sixties
now, none of it had gone soft.

Reeves was riding toward the sheriff's office when three
men did just that. They stepped into the street, wearing
guns, and barred his way.

He reined in and stared at them from beneath his battered hat. Reeves had a bandolier across his chest, a gun in a holster, and a Winchester in his scabbard.

"One of them bodies better not be our brother Clem, Reeves," one of the men said. Reeves knew these were the Ferris brothers. The spokesman was the older brother, John Ferris. One of the men he had behind him, tied to a horse, was indeed their younger brother, Clem.

"Ferris, your brother knew what he and his partner were doin' when they decided to rob stagecoaches and kill folks. He also knew he was gonna have ta deal with me sooner than later."

"And you knew if you went after our brother," Ferris said, "that you'd have to deal with us, sooner or later."

"I was kinda hopin' for later," Bass Reeves said frankly.

"So Clem is back there, on one of them horses?" John Ferris asked.

"He is."

"And he's dead?"

"As dead as can be."

"The nigger killed Clem," one of the other brothers said. His name was Jake.

"He's got to die for that, Johnny," a third brother, Jerry, said.

"You hear my brothers, Reeves?" Ferris asked.

"I hear 'em."

"Whadaya think?"

"I think none of you better think about killin' a U.S. marshal."

"We're thinkin' about killin' a nigger," one of the brothers said. "That's all."

"Come on, Johnny," Jake said. "He's just a nigger."

"A nigger with a badge," Reeves said.

"A nigger with a badge," John Ferris said, "is still just a nigger, Reeves. Get off your horse."

Reeves eyed the three men, then saw two more men step into the street.

"More brothers?"

"Cousins," Ferris said. "They don't like havin' relatives shot down by a nigger any more than we do."

"Five against one," Reeves said. "That sound like fair odds to you?"

"What odds did you give our brother?" Jake demanded.

"As a matter of fact," Reeves said, "I was down two to one."

"But you still killed him and his partner, Ames," John Ferris said.

"Your brother wasn't very good with a gun, Ferris," Reeves said.

"Well, me and my other brothers—and my cousins—don't have that problem, Reeves," John Ferris said. "We're very good with our guns."

"Well, so am I," Reeves said, "but five to one—"

"Those are the best odds yer gonna get," Jake Ferris said, "fer killin' our brother."

Bass Reeves looked around him. They had attracted quite a crowd of onlookers, lining both sides of the street, but he knew he wouldn't be able to depend on any of them for help.

He was on his own.

Or so he thought.

TWO

"You gents mind if I take a hand?"

All eyes fell on the man who stepped into the street from behind Bass Reeves, making it clear he was not with the Ferris family.

The man moved toward the center of the street and stopped.

"I mean, it would even up the odds a little, wouldn't it?" the man asked.

"Mister," John Ferris said, "this ain't none of your affair."

"Oh, I know that," the man said, "but you know, I never could just stand by and watch a man be outgunned. Especially not a lawman."

"But . . ." Jake stammered, "but . . . he's just a nigger."

The man held up his index finger and corrected Jake.

"Nigger with a badge."

"Look, mister," John Ferris said again, "we got no beef with you."

"That's okay," Clint Adams said, "I got a beef with a bunch of morons ganging up on one lawman."

Ferris frowned.

"You a lawman, too, is that it?"

"No," Clint said, "not a lawman, just a concerned citizen."

"A citizen who's lookin' ta get killed," Jerry said. "John, I say we kill him, too."

But John Ferris was still curious about who this fella was and why he'd want to take a hand in another man's fight.

"Come on, John," one of his cousins called out. "We ain't got all day. Call it."

"You boys still wanna go on with this?" Bass Reeves asked. "Or you done forgot about me?"

"We ain't forgot about you, nigger," John Ferris said. "Get down off your horse, or we'll shoot you off it."

"Gimme a minute now," Reeves said. "I ain't as young as I used ta be."

Clint studied the five men in the street. The three brothers were wearing holsters, while the two cousins were holding rifles. Reeves dismounted, left his rifle on his saddle. All he had was his holstered pistol, but Clint knew he was proficient with it.

Reeves held his hands out to the Ferris family and said, "Just let me get somebody to take these horses off the street."

"I'll take 'em," a man said, stepping into the street. "No point in good horses catchin' lead."

'Course not, Reeves thought, *but no problem for a black man to catch some.*

"You ready, Reeves?" John Ferris asked.

"Whatcha askin' him if he's ready for, Johnny," one of his cousins asked. "Jesus, shoot the black fucker down already!"

"It's gotta be fair and square!" Ferris yelled.

"Jesus . . ." the man said from behind Ferris.

"Okay, let's do this," Clint said. "I was on my way to get a drink."

"You don't seem worried to be facin' five men, mister," John Ferris said.

"Believe me, Ferris," Clint said, "I've faced worse odds than this and walked away, and that's what I intend to do today. Like your idiot cousin says, let's get it over with."

"Son of a—" the idiot cousin said, drawing his gun.

Clint drew quickly, shot the man down in the street, and holstered his gun before any of the other Ferris boys had a chance to move.

"Uh, oh," Clint said, "your odds just went down."

"What the—" Jake Ferris said. "Did you see that, Johnny?"

"I didn't even have a chance to flinch," Jerry said.

"You're lucky," Clint said. "If you had flinched, you'd be dead, too."

"Who the hell are you, mister?" John Ferris asked.

"My name's Clint Adams."

A murmur went up from the crowd and the color drained from John Ferris's face.

"Th-The Gunsmith?" he asked.

"That's right."

"Jesus, Johnny," his other cousin demanded, "what'd you get us into?"

"Why you wanna make this your fight, Adams?" John Ferris asked. "We got nothin' against you."

"Marshal Reeves happens to be a friend of mine," Clint said. "Can't just stand by and watch a friend get shot down in the street, can I?"

"I don't—"

"You know, Ferris, this has gone on too long already,"

Clint said. "You and your family aren't going to draw now, so why don't you turn and walk away?"

"That's our brother on that horse," he said.

"And that's your cousin dead in the street," Clint said. "You want to join them?"

"I don't wanna join them, Johnny," Jerry said.

"Me, neither," Jake said.

"Take your dead and bury them, Ferris," Clint said. "This is all over."

Bass Reeves turned to the man who was holding the horses and waved him over. He pointed to one of the horses and the man walked that animal over to John Ferris and handed him the reins.

"This ain't right, Adams," Ferris said. "This ain't right, you sidin' with a black man against yer own."

"Believe me, Ferris," Clint said, "you and your boys aren't my own, and I'm grateful for that."

For a moment Clint thought that comment might make the man draw, but then Ferris turned and led the horses away while the other boys picked up the dead cousin and carried him away, too.

Clint walked over to Bass Reeves, who put his hand out to shake.

"Sure glad you come along when you did, Clint."

"Bass," Clint said, "you sure know how to show a guest a good time."

THREE

Bass Reeves had to check in with the local sheriff as well as the judge, but he agreed to meet Clint in the saloon in an hour for a drink.

The street cleared off, many of the men moving into one or another of the saloons that lined Main Street. Clint, who had only just arrived about half an hour before Reeves rode in, had only had time to see to his horse and check into a hotel before the action commenced.

"How about a steak somewhere?" he'd asked Reeves.

"I know just the place," Reeves had said.

So Clint went into the Red Ace Saloon and ordered a beer while he waited for Bass Reeves to join him.

"You took a big chance out there, mister," the bartender said.

"You think so?" Clint asked.

"Lot of white men in this town mighta stepped into the street to face that nigger."

"That nigger is a deputy U.S. marshal," Clint said. "And he's a man. He's also a friend of mine. I don't appreciate your tone, so why don't you take it on down the line. I'll call you if I need anything."

"Hey, I was just makin' conversation."

"Make it with somebody else."

Grumbling, the bartender moved away to the far end of the bar.

"He's just sayin' what a lot of folks are thinkin'," a voice said from behind him.

He turned and saw a man wearing a sheriff's badge standing there.

"That how you feel?" Clint asked. "You wear a badge. Is Reeves a man first, a lawman first, or just a black man?"

"Don't matter what I think," the sheriff said. "He takes a chance every time he brings a white man in—especially when they're tied to their saddle."

"He's doing his job," Clint said. "You should've been doing yours out there."

"My job don't mean I gotta take my life in my hands by standin' with Bass Reeves," the sheriff said.

"What's your name?"

"Bates."

"Well, Sheriff Bates," Clint said, "seems to me you and the bartender have got a lot in common."

"Oh, yeah? What's that?"

"You'd both be better off down at that end of the bar."

FOUR

When Reeves walked in, Clint could feel the attitude in the place change. Seemed most of the men in the saloon were only used to seeing a black man in a saloon to swamp it out.

"You get warned?" Reeves asked Clint, joining him at the bar.

"Yeah," Clint said. "The bartender and the sheriff. You want a drink?"

"They won't serve me," Reeves said. "They'd have to throw out the glass. Gets expensive."

Clint called the bartender over.

"A beer for my friend," he said.

"But—"

"Draw him a beer . . . now."

The bartender hesitated, looked around for help, and when none was forthcoming he drew Reeves a beer, slammed it down on the bar hard enough to spill some of it, and stalked off.

"Why do you bother, Bass?" Clint asked. "I mean, wearing the badge."

Reeves sipped his beer and then looked down at the badge on his chest.

"Clint, this here badge is the only thing in my life that don't see color first."

"Okay," Clint said, "I can understand that."

"What brings you to Paris?" Reeves asked.

"Just passing through, if you can believe that," Clint said.

"Well, why don't we get that steak and catch up?" Reeves asked.

"We going to have trouble finding a place that will serve you a steak?" Clint asked.

"No, sir," Reeves said, "we ain't."

When they entered the small café, Clint could see why Reeves was sure there'd be no trouble.

"Why Mr. Bass Reeves," the black waitress said, "you come here and give me a hug, boy."

Reeves hugged the woman, who was at least thirty years younger than he was.

"Your mama in the kitchen, Violet?" Reeves asked.

"And where else would she be at this time of the day?" The woman gave Clint a frank look and asked, "Who's your friend?"

"Violet, this is Clint Adams," Reeves said. "He just saved my no good, lazy black ass in the street."

"Saved you?"

"Seems the Ferris boys wanted to shoot some holes in me for bringin' in their brother."

"Clem?"

Reeves nodded.

"Dead?"

"His choice," Reeves said.

"You boys sit yourselves down," she said. "I'll have Mama fix you two steaks. Mr. Adams, I'm obliged to you for savin' this no good lout's ass."

"My pleasure, ma'am."

"Don't you be callin' me ma'am," she said. "My name's Violet. You use it."

"Okay, Violet."

As she walked away, Clint watched her with pleasure. She was a handsome woman, there was no doubt, and she'd probably be even better-looking when she wasn't in the middle of a workday.

"Are you and she—"

"Her mama is Nellie's cousin," Reeves said. Nellie was his wife, Clint knew.

"So that kind of makes her your . . ."

"I dunno," Reeves said, "but we're related."

"How many kids you got now?"

"We got ten young'ns," Reeves said. "Five boys and five girls."

"I don't know how you found the time to have that many kids, Bass."

"I got me a good woman, Clint," Reeves said. "Somethin' you could use."

"Not me," Clint said. "I gave up long ago any thoughts of settling down."

"The right woman could change your mind."

"You might be right," Clint said, "but it hasn't come close to happening yet."

Violet came back with a pot of coffee and two cups.

"Your steaks is on, and here's some good, strong coffee."

"Just the way I like it," Clint said.

"Yeah, you look like a man who likes things strong . . . coffee, horses . . . women."

She turned and walked off before he could comment.

"I'm tellin' ya," Reeves said, grinning, "the right woman . . ."

"Drink your coffee, Reeves."

FIVE

The steak was perfectly prepared, as were the vegetables and rolls that came with it. While they ate, they caught up on each other's lives, since they hadn't seen one another in some years and had only been able to depend on newspaper accounts and rumor to keep track. Afterward, they had another pot of coffee and Violet's mother, Viola, came out to say hello to Reeves and meet Clint.

"I heard you saved this worthless ol' man's ass," Viola said.

"Somebody had to," Clint said.

"Well, I'm sure my cousin Nellie will be very grateful." She looked down at Reeves. "Is you goin' home to see your wife and children anytime soon?"

"Soon, Viola," Reeves said, "very soon."

She slapped him on the shoulder and said, "A pleasure meetin' you, Mr. Adams."

If Viola was what Violet was going to look like in thirty years or so, some man was going to be very lucky. Clint wondered if Viola had a husband at the moment.

"Ma'am," Clint said, "if you don't mind, I might come back for another meal or two while I'm here."

"That'd be right fine," she said, "even if you come without the marshal, there, we'll be sure ta treat you well."

"Thank you."

As she left, Clint looked at Reeves and asked, "Is that true? You going home to see your wife and kids?"

"Not exactly," the lawman said.

"Why not?"

"I just got another assignment from the judge."

"Can't he give it to somebody else?"

"Don't want him to," Reeves said.

"Why not?"

"Because of who the warrants are for."

"And who's that?"

"You ever heard of Nat Love?"

"Black cowboy, right?"

"Right," Reeves said, "one of the most famous."

"That's who you have to track?"

"Not him, but others like him," Reeves said. "A lot of the cow outfits are havin' hard times and they've let a lot of men go."

"Let me guess," Clint said. "Most of the cowpokes they've let go are black."

"Right, and they're not happy about it."

"So they've turned owlhoot?"

"Looks like."

"So why do you have to be the one to go after them?" Clint asked.

"Because if a white man goes after them, they'll come back dead."

"Like Clem Ferris and his partner?"

"They didn't gimme no choice."

"And what about these boys?" Clint asked. "What if they don't give you a choice."

"Point is," Reeves said, "they'll have a better chance with me."

"Don't go getting yourself killed giving them a chance, Bass."

"I might," Reeves admitted. "Them bein' black, I might let down some and get killed. Ya never know."

Clint frowned across the table at his friend.

"What are you trying to pull?"

"I ain't tryin' ta pull nothin', Clint."

"Oh, yeah," Clint said, "I don't remember you ever talking about maybe getting yourself killed."

"Well," Reeves said, "I'm sixty damn years old. Fella slows down, ya know."

"I didn't see you slowing down any when those five men wanted to face you in the street."

"See there?" Reeves said. "That's just the kind of fool decision that could get me killed. If you hadn't stepped in—"

"I hadn't stepped in you might have gunned all five of those men without any help from me, and you know it."

"Naw, I don't know it," Reeves said. "One of them crackers probably woulda winged me."

"Bass," Clint said, "are you asking me to go with you to track these black cowboys down, or are you trying to fool me into offering?"

"Well," Reeves said, "I reckon what I'm tryin' to do is get you to volunteer."

"What? No offer of a badge?"

"I don't think the judge would go for that, Clint,"

Reeves said. "He don't just hand badges out to anybody, ya know."

"Really?" Clint asked. "From where I'm sitting you really couldn't tell."

SIX

The six black men sat around the fire, sullenly eating their beans and swigging water from their canteens. They were all in their thirties, children of slaves who had grown to be free men, if you can call working your fingers to the bone being free. They all had them, work-hardened hands and sun-ravaged faces. Some looked forty, some fifty, but none of them was over thirty-five. It was hard work that aged you, whether you were free or not.

But now there was no hard work. They had all been let go by their cow outfits, and now they stole what they could, robbing stagecoaches, travelers, even a trading post or two.

"My folks would die if they saw me now," George Washington said. "They named me after the first president because they wanted me to grow up and be somebody. So who do I become? A bank robber."

"And what was dey?" Adam Lee asked. "Dey was slaves."

"But they was proud."

"But we free."

"Don't feel likes we free," said Ben Jones. "Don't feel like it a'tall."

Adam Lee stood up. He was the unofficial leader of this ragtag group of ex-cowhands turned robbers.

"We doin' what we gots ta do to feed ourselves and our families," he shouted at them. "Who sayin' dat ain't somet'ing ta be proud of?"

"Feedin' yer family is fine," George said, "but there's something to how you do it."

"No, dey ain't," Lee said. "You jes' do it or ya don't. Ain't no in between. Ya eats, or ya dies."

The other men nodded their heads. They were with Lee on this.

"Well, you know the law ain't gonna stand for this," George said.

"And ya know who dey gonna sends for us," Jones said.

"I know," George said. "I know they'll be sendin' Bass Reeves afta us, and I don't care. I got to do what I got to do."

"And Bass Reeves gon' do what he gots ta do," Jones said.

Lee took out his worn peacemaker and said, "Ah puts a bullet in Bass Reeves's head, he don't do nuthin' no mo'."

With that he sat down, picked up his plate of beans, and started eating again.

"South of the Red River," Reeves said to Clint. "They wouldn't go north. There's nothin' for them there."

"Might be better pickings there," Clint pointed out.

"Better, maybe," Reeves said, "but not easier. Plus, their families are here. No, they ain't gonna go north of the Red River."

"Still leaves a lot of ground to be covered," Clint said.

They were back in the saloon, a beer each in front of

them—another glass to be thrown away, and that tickled Clint. They had taken a back table and were careful to watch each other's backs.

"I figure we head out at first light and head south," Reeves said. "They hit a stage over near Sherman a couple of days ago. They're gonna hafta take some supplies to their families before they go out and pull another job."

"So if we find their families, we find them. This is your territory. Where do you suppose they've got them stashed?"

"I got a couple of ideas," Reeves said. "I'll give it some more thought overnight."

"Okay. What do we do about supplies?"

"I usually just carry what I can on my saddle," Reeves said.

"I'm the same way. Too many supplies—and a packhorse—just slow you down."

"We'll need some coffee and beans, some beef jerky, and some ammunition," Reeves said. "The judge gimme a voucher I can use at the general store, so I'll pick that stuff up."

"I'll bet they really like that," Clint said. "Maybe I should go with you."

"Naw, I do this all the time. They don't like that I get supplies, but they give 'em ta me."

"I don't know, Bass," Clint said. "I'd be really tempted just to tell these people to keep their own laws enforced."

"Ain't their law, Clint," Reeves said. "The law's for everybody."

"I'm going to stop arguing with you, Bass," Clint said. "Your points are too good."

SEVEN

Clint and Reeves split up and agreed to meet in front of the livery stable at first light. Reeves would have whatever supplies they were going to carry, and by that time both men would have examined their weapons to be sure they were in working order.

Clint went back to the Red Ace to relax over a beer. There were a couple of poker games going on, but he stayed away. They were penny-ante, and all of the players were bad. They were just passing the time, too.

The bartender glared at him every chance he got, but Clint ignored him, just as he paid no attention to the other patrons looking at him. He didn't know if they were staring because of who he was or because of who he was friends with, and he didn't particularly care.

After his beer, Clint left the saloon and started back to his hotel. There was a dining room there and he was ready for some supper. On the way, though, he ran into one of the few people in town he knew.

"Hello, Violet."

She'd been hurrying along and had to look right at him before she realized who he was.

"Oh, hello, Mr. Adams."

"My name is Clint," he said. "Remember?"

"Yes, Clint."

"Where are you hurrying to?" he asked.

"Back to work. Mama's gonna need me for the supper rush. What about you?"

"I was actually going to go to my hotel to eat," he admitted.

"Oh, no," she said, "the food there is terrible! You come with me and we'll fix you a good meal."

"I didn't want to take advantage of my friendship with Bass—"

"Never mind," she said. "We'll feed you and you'll pay the tab. How's that?"

"That sounds good to me."

She smiled, her face lighting up and becoming beautiful. "Come on."

She grabbed his hand and pulled him toward her mother's café.

Bass Reeves entered the judge's chamber and stood in front of his boss's desk.

"Back so soon, Deputy?" the judge asked. He leaned back in his chair, his bulk making it squeak. The best man Reeves had ever worked for had been Judge Isaac Parker, but his present employer came pretty close.

"Sir," Reeves said, "I just wanted to tell ya I'll be leavin' first thing in the morning."

"To go after that black cowboy gang?"

"Yes, sir."

"What changed your mind?"

"A friend of mine convinced me they'd be better off with me chasin' them than some white deputy," Reeves said. He didn't bother telling the judge that it had actually happened the other way around.

"My deputies are all good men, Reeves," the judge said. "Some of them even worked with you in Judge Parker's court."

"I know that, sir," Reeves said. "I just think this is best."

"Well, as a matter of fact, I do, too," the judge said. "I'm glad you changed your mind."

"Yes, sir."

Reeves turned to leave.

"The word we have is that there are at least half a dozen of them," the judge said. "You might want to take some help. One of your colleagues, maybe?"

Reeves didn't have any colleagues. The white deputies resented him, even the ones he had worked with in Judge Parker's court.

"I can handle it, sir."

"Yes, you usually can," the judge said. "What about what happened in the street today?"

"The Ferris brothers?" Reeves smiled. "They changed their minds."

"So I heard," the judge said. "You had some help."

"Yes, sir."

"Clint Adams, wasn't it?"

"Yes, sir."

"He a friend of yours?"

"Yes, sir."

"Maybe he'd be willing to help you."

"Yes, sir," Reeves said. "That's possible."

The judge studied him for a moment, then said, "All right, Deputy. What you do is up to you."

"Yes, sir."

Reeves left the judge's chamber.

EIGHT

Clint figured out that Violet had been being sarcastic about the supper rush. There were a few diners in the place, but they were all black. No white faces anywhere. She took him to a table where he sat with his back to the wall and brought him a cup of coffee.

"Another steak?" she asked.

"Something not as . . . big."

"A bowl of stew?" she asked. "Mama makes a great stew."

"Okay," he said, "A bowl of stew."

She smiled and said, "Comin' up."

There were only seven tables in the whole place. Aside from his, another one was taken by a black man and woman in their fifties. They kept glancing at him, but when he'd look at them they'd avert their eyes.

When Violet passed by Clint's table, he said, "Do you know that older couple?"

"Sure, that's Hattie Ray and her husband Walter."

"Are they nice people?"

"Of course they are."

"Are they friends of Bass Reeves?"

"No, I don't think Bass knows them."

"Well, would you tell them that I'm not a bad man?" Clint asked.

Violet laughed, showing very white teeth.

"Are they starin' at you?"

"Just the opposite," he said. "They're . . . stealing glances, and then looking away. I'd like them to relax and enjoy their meal. In fact, tell them I'll pay for their meal."

"I'll tell them you're a nice man," she said, "but they're proud people. They'll wanna pay for their own meal."

"Okay," Clint said. "I don't want to offend anyone. I just don't want them waiting for me to shoot them, or something."

"I'll tell them you're harmless," she said, then added, "or maybe that's a lie."

She arched an eyebrow at him, then went over to the other table and spoke to the couple. From that point on, they enjoyed their meal and didn't look over at him.

Violet brought him his bowl of stew and, as promised, it was wonderful.

"Are they bothering you now?" she asked with an amused smile.

"No," he said, "you can let them stay."

Now she laughed out loud and went back to her mother's kitchen.

An hour later he was still there. The older couple had gone, no one else had come in, and he was sitting with both Violet and Viola—two beautiful women, mother and daughter. As it turned out Viola's husband—Violet's father—had died several years earlier.

"This café is all we have now," Viola said. "We're tryin' ta make it work together, but . . ."

"What Mama's tryin' ta say is"—Violet put her hand over her mother's—"we're not gonna make it unless we can get some white people to start eatin' here."

"I don't see why they won't," Clint said. "The food is delicious."

"Folks around here don't take to black folks," Violet said. "You saw what happened today with Bass. As long as he wears a badge . . ."

"Wait a minute," Clint said. "Are you telling me that people don't come here because they know you're related to Bass?"

"That's just one of the reasons," Viola said.

"A big one," Violet added.

"Do you think if Bass gave up his badge things would change?"

"Not really," Viola said, "but I would never ask him ta do such a thing. Not for us. For his own family, maybe, but not for us."

"He'll never give up that badge," Violet said. "It's his reason for livin'. He'll be wearin' a badge when he's eighty, you mark my words."

"I just hope his sons don't follow in his footsteps," Viola said. "It's hard enough bein' a lawman without bein' a black lawman."

At that point an elderly black man entered, and when he saw Clint he started to back out. Violet jumped up and grabbed him, spoke to him briefly, and then led him to a table.

"You want the usual, Eldred?" Viola asked, getting up.

"Yes'm," the old man said. "Thank ya."

"Comin' up. Oh, Eldred, this here's Mr. Adams. He's a friend of ours."

"How do," Eldred said.

"Fine," Clint said, "I do just fine, Eldred."

He wished he could say the same for Bass Reeves and his family.

NINE

Clint ended up staying until closing, when Viola shooed both him and Violet out of the place.

"I don't need no help cleanin' my own kitchen," she told them. "Mr. Adams, you be a gentleman and walk my girl home, now, you hear?"

"Yes, ma'am."

"Oh, Mama."

"You hush up, child, and go. I'll see you directly, when I'm done here."

"Good night, Viola."

"Good night, Mr. Adams."

Violet kissed her mother's cheek and said, "I'll see you later, Mama."

Clint and Violet stepped outside and Viola locked the door behind them. It was still light out and Clint noticed a white couple across the street staring at them disapprovingly.

"Is this going to be a problem for you?" he asked her.

"What, you walkin' me home?" she asked. "It'll be a town scandal, and I don't give a damn." To illustrate her point she linked her arm in his. It was his left arm, so he let her do it.

The Ferris brothers spent the day in a small saloon in the south end of town, just the three of them, sitting at a table and drinking.

John, Jerry, and Jake Ferris were brooding. Their brother Clem was at the undertaker's, their cousins had left town, not wanting to be around while Clint Adams was in town.

"That son of a bitch Adams," Jake Ferris seethed. "If it weren't for him, we would've taken care of that nigger."

"We still can," John said. "we just gotta catch him without Adams."

"Yeah, but if we kill 'im," Jerry asked, "is the Gunsmith gonna come after us?"

"What does that matter?" John demanded. "He killed our brother."

"Clem was an idiot," Jake said. "What the hell was he doin' with that partner of his anyway?"

"It don't matter," John said again. "Nothin' matters but that he was our brother and Bass Reeves killed him. I say we find Reeves and make him pay."

"Well . . . okay, Johnny," Jake said, "but then I say we get outta town."

"Amen to that!" Jerry said.

"Let's go," John said, getting up.

The three of them lurched toward the saloon doors.

Bass Reeves missed his kids, all ten of them. After this was over he was going to go back home to his ranch, see his wife and kids, and consider how much longer he wanted to wear a badge.

But who was he kidding? Without his badge what was

he? With it they called him a "nigger with a badge," so without it that just made him another nigger, right? He knew he'd be wearing a badge until he dropped dead. They'd have to unpin it from his shirt. Or maybe they'd bury him with it. Wouldn't that be something? Being put in the ground with that hunk of tin still stuck to his shirt? Since Nellie was younger than he was, he was going to have to tell her that was what he wanted.

Some of the deputies hung around the building where the judge's chambers were. There was a room just outside the jail where they'd sit and drink coffee and swap stories. Reeves had never felt welcome there, so whenever he needed a place to sit or sleep, he'd go into the cell block and pick out an empty cell.

He wasn't ready to sleep, though, and he wasn't hungry. That steak was still sitting heavily with him. He decided he'd take a walk, maybe stop in one of the smaller saloons where they didn't care what color you were. Places like that were very few, but there were a couple saloons where all they cared about was what you wanted to drink.

Reeves left the cell block, walked past two of his colleagues without exchanging a word, and stepped out onto the street.

Clint and Violet strolled through the street as she directed him to the south end of town.

"There ain't many black people livin' here," she said, "but what there is live here."

As they got closer, he could see the buildings getting more and more run-down and in disrepair. They also passed some small saloons that seemed pretty quiet.

"Black folks also drink at this end of town," she said.

At that moment the batwings of one saloon opened and three white men came staggering out.

"And some whites," she said.

As the men straightened up and stepped into the street, Clint recognized them.

The Ferris boys.

TEN

Bass Reeves saw the three men exit the saloon, then saw Clint Adams walking across the street with Violet. He recognized the Ferris boys and knew if they were drunk they might not back down this time.

He quickened his pace.

"Well, lookee what we got here," John Ferris shouted. "Is that the famous Gunsmith, walkin' down the street with a nigger gal on his arm?"

"Looks like it to me," Jerry Ferris said.

"I guess Mr. Gunsmith likes him some dark meat, huh?" Jake asked.

"You boys are drunk," Clint said. "Drunk is a bad way to die."

Any thought of backing down this time had long since died in an alcoholic haze. Just in the time it took the three men to walk from their table to the door, they suddenly became invincible.

"Clint—" Violet said.

"Don't worry, Violet," he said. "It'll be okay."

"I don't want you to do nothin' on my account."

"Don't worry," he said again. "Anything I do will be on my account."

Reeves saw the three men step into the street, heard them shouting at Clint and Violet. None of them were making a move toward their guns, though, not at this point.

He was almost on them and shouted, "Hold it!"

The three Ferris boys, as well as Clint and Violet, all looked Bass Reeves's way.

"It's him, Johnny," Jerry Ferris shouted. "It's the nigger!"

"Forget Adams," Jake shouted. "Get the nigger!"

All three men went for their guns.

Bass Reeves saw the three Ferris brothers reach for their guns, all of their attention on him. He grabbed for his own gun, cleared leather smoothly, and fired.

Clint couldn't let Reeves face the three men alone this time any more than he could have earlier that day, so he pushed Violet away from him and drew his gun.

"Hey, Ferris!"

Only one Ferris brother even heard Clint shout, and that was Jake. Abruptly, he turned to face Clint just as the Gunsmith pulled the trigger twice. Both bullets struck Jake Ferris in the chest and put him down in the street.

John and Jerry Ferris both drew on Bass Reeves, but even if they hadn't been drunk they never would have been fast enough. Reeves was a very deliberate man with a gun, and once given no choice he was deadly accurate. He shot Jerry in the heart, then turned the gun on John and did the same. In the blink of an eye all three Ferris brothers were down on their backs, and soon they'd be joining their brother Clem at the undertaker's.

Clint and Reeves came together with the Ferris brothers at their feet.

"I guess it had to happen," Clint said.

"Yeah," Reeves said, "all it took was a little whiskey."

"Judging from the smell coming up from these fellers, I'd say it was a lot of whiskey."

Both men ejected their spent shells and replaced them with live loads before returning their guns to their holsters. At that point Violet came over to join them, hugging her upper arms as if she were cold.

Men were coming out of the saloons little by little. This part of town had seen just about everything there was to see, and there was no guarantee that the action would even attract the sheriff's attention.

"I'll wait here and see if the sheriff shows up," Reeves said. "You take Violet home."

"I'll get her home and then come back and wait with you," Clint said. "We can support each other's story."

Reeves shrugged.

"Don't look like there was any other witnesses gonna argue the point."

"Nevertheless," Clint said, "I'll be back."

Reeves shrugged again, then turned to urge the onlookers to go back into the saloon. There was nothing left to see.

ELEVEN

"Clint, you and Bass ain't gonna be in trouble because of this, are you?" Violet asked when they reached the small shack she shared with her mother.

"No," Clint said. "They drew first, and Bass is a lawman."

"If there's trouble I can be a witness."

Clint took hold of her shoulders and said, "Violet, you don't have to do anything but get some rest. I've got to get back to Bass now."

"A-all right."

As he took his hands away from her shoulders, she impulsively hugged him. He enjoyed the fleeting feeling of her warm body against his, and then she was gone, closing the door behind her.

He turned and hurried back to wait with Reeves for the local law.

When Clint rejoined Bass Reeves, he found him in the company of the local sheriff. The three bodies were still on the ground.

"Clint, this here's Sheriff Bates."

"We met," Clint said, "although not formally."

"Seems like you two couldn't avoid these fellas, huh?" Bates asked.

"That's the way it was, Sheriff," Clint said. "They didn't give us much of a chance."

"Well, I'll have somebody clean these boys up, take 'em over to the undertaker with their brother. My guess is the judge is gonna back you, Reeves, for gunnin' three white men."

"Two," Clint said. "I killed one of them—and what's there to back? All Bass did was his job."

"That ain't exactly true," the sheriff said congenially. He was a bland-looking man in his thirties who seemed very comfortable with his lot in life. "See, now if I had killed these jaspers I woulda been doin' my job, because I'm the town sheriff. I'm the law here, not Bass Reeves, or any of the other deputies, who work for the judge. So if I wanted to lock Reeves up for shootin' these fellas I could. My point is, the judge would just let 'im out—again."

"Okay," Clint said, "you made your point."

"I got one more point to make."

"What's that?" Clint asked.

"I could lock you up for killin' a man."

"If you wanted to do that," Clint said, turning to face the man squarely, "you'd have to take my gun, Sheriff. Frankly, I don't think you're man enough to do that."

The two men studied each other for a moment, then Sheriff Bates averted his eyes and said, "Well, um, I was just makin' a point."

"Are you done making points now?" Clint asked.

"Uh, sure."

"Come on, Bass," Clint said. "I'll buy you a drink."

"Sure thing."

They both walked away from the sheriff, who started looking around for some men to move the bodies.

"Hey," he called, "send me some men outta that saloon, will ya?"

Clint tossed a wave over his shoulder.

"Whiskey?" he asked as they entered.

"Beer," Reeves said.

While Clint got two beers from the bar, Reeves picked out some men and sent them outside to help the sheriff. By the time he was done, the saloon was almost empty.

"Nobody's looking at us here," Clint said, sitting down with Reeves.

"Nobody on this side of town cares what color you are," Reeves said.

"Sounds like this might be the side of town to be on, then."

"Don't believe it," Reeves said. "They also walk around dead men in the street here. Actually, nobody cares about nothin' over here. They all been livin' with despair their whole lives."

"Including Violet and her mother?"

"They been livin' with it a few years now," he said. "They had it pretty good when Viola's man was alive, but now it's just the two of them. My Nellie keeps tellin' them to come live with us, but they's proud."

"Yeah," Clint said, "I'm running into a lot of that lately. What were you doing on this side of town anyway, Bass?"

"I suddenly got hungry," he said. "A man can eat here without bein' stared at."

"They serve food here?" Clint asked.

"They do."

"Then let's get you something to eat," Clint said. "I want you at full strength tomorrow when we head out."

"Don't you worry," Bass Reeves said, "I'll be at full strength."

TWELVE

Clint went back to his room after having a beer with Bass Reeves. Reeves told him he'd be spending the night in one of the empty cells and rejected Clint's offer to get him a room in the hotel. They agreed to meet in front of the livery at first light.

In his room Clint worked on his rifle and his pistol, cleaning both and making sure they were both in proper working order. He had put them both away, satisfied that they would perform when needed, when there was a knock on the door. Quickly, he drew his gun from his holster. There was no way of knowing how many friends the Ferris boys might have had in town. Or it might even be their idiotic cousins again.

He stood to the side so no one could shoot him through the door and asked, "Who is it?"

"Clint? It's Violet. Can I come in, please?"

He opened the door, saw Violet standing there with her hands clasped in front of her.

"Violet, is everything all right?"

"I-I thought it was."

"Come inside before somebody sees you." He grabbed her hand, pulled her inside. He looked both ways in the hall, and then closed the door.

"You can shoot me if you want to," she said, "but I had to come."

"What's it all about?" he asked. He walked to the bed, picked up the holster, put the gun in it, and hung the holster and gun on the bedpost.

"I-I got back home, started to get ready for bed, and then I thought about what happened," she said. "I thought how Bass, or you, could've been killed."

"That's something he and I live with every day," Clint said. "It's nothing new."

"It's new to me," she said. "I expect to be mistreated every day—I've grown up with that—but not killed. How can you live with something like that?"

"It's something you have to learn, that's for sure," he said.

"Well, all I could think was that we've just met, me and you, and before I know it you could be dead."

"Well," he said, "that's not likely—"

"But it is, it is likely that I may never see you again," she said. "We heard you talkin', we know you're goin' with Bass after those black cowboys."

"Yeah, I'm sorry about that," he said. "Actually, them being black has nothing to do with it—"

"No, it doesn't, you fool," she said. "It's not about them, it's about you and me . . ."

"You and . . . me?"

"If I don't do this now, I may never get the chance again."

She was wearing a simple cotton dress, which she hadn't

been wearing at the café. There she'd been wearing a blouse and a skirt that were billowy, hiding her body, but this dress made it plain she was wearing nothing underneath. She had small breasts, but they were hard, with prominent nipples he could see right through the fabric. But now she reached behind her, undid something, and suddenly the dress was down around her ankles.

She had a beautiful body, chocolate brown and not an ounce of fat on her. A flat belly, slender thighs and legs. Her nipples were dark brown, even darker than her skin. Her hair was long, coming down to her shoulders, and she had a lovely, long neck.

"You're beautiful, Violet," he said, thickly, "but . . . does your mother know you're here?"

"My mother understands," she said. Then she giggled. "In fact, I think my mother would like to be here. She's probably closer to your age than I am—"

"Don't tell me how old you are," he said.

"—but it's too bad for her," she went on, "because I got here first."

She came closer and he could smell her, a combination of cooking smells from the café, her own musky skin, and the tangy smell from between her legs that told him she was ready.

Her slender arm came up and she laced her long, tapered fingers behind his neck and pulled him down into a deep, wet kiss that took their breath away.

"Oh, yes," she said, against his lips, "this was a good idea, after all . . ."

She would get no argument from him on that count.

He scooped her up in his arms, carried her to the bed, and set her down easily. Then he quickly undressed and joined her on the mattress.

She grabbed him to her eagerly. Violet didn't want to waste any time. She just wanted him inside of her, and he was only to happy to oblige. She was so wet, he slid in easily, to the hilt, causing her to catch her breath, and then they started to move together, at first each with a rhythm of their own, but gradually they found one that suited them both, and then they settled in for a long night . . .

THIRTEEN

"Have you ever been with a black girl before?" she asked, her head nestled on his shoulder.

"Once or twice."

"This is my first time with a white man."

"And what's the verdict?"

She licked his shoulder and said, "You taste different."

"Bad?"

"Kinda . . . funny."

"Funny?"

"Funny, in a good way."

"Well, you're kind of skinny," he said, and then added, "in a good way."

"I didn't hear no complaints a little while ago," she said.

"Oh, believe me," he said, "I have no complaints, but I'm kind of worried about you."

"Me? Oh, I have got no complaints."

"I mean, I'm worried about your reputation," he said. "The desk clerk must have seen you come up—"

"Are you crazy?" she asked, cutting him off. "I don't got

no reputation in this town, Clint. I'm black." She held her arm in front of him. "In case you ain't noticed?"

"I noticed," he said. "I was taking a real long, good look."

"That reminds me," she said. "I was so anxious to get you inside me that I didn't take a good long look at my first white man. Do you mind?"

"Be my guest."

She sat up, stared down at him, ran her hand over his chest and belly, then slid her hand lower, wrapped her fingers in his pubic hair before moving on to his penis, which she lifted in her hand.

"Mmm . . ." she said.

He started to swell.

"Oh, my, are you ready again?"

"Violet," he said, "you're holding me in your hand. What man wouldn't be ready?"

"Oh, my, there it goes . . ." She leaned over so she could examine him more closely. "My God, but that's real pretty, ain't it?"

"That's not for me to say," he replied, "or agree with."

"Well, take my word for it," she said, "you got the prettiest pecker I ever seen."

She held it in one hand while she stroked it with the other, first along the top, then the underside. When her finger touched the spot just below the head he jumped and she laughed.

"Sensitive?"

"Very."

"Hmm . . ."

She continued to examine him, then leaned over and touched that sensitive spot again, but this time with her tongue. He jumped again and before he could settle back down, she took the spongy head into her mouth, sucked it wetly, and then released it.

"Oh, God . . ." he said.

"You liked that?"

"I loved it!"

"Ya know," she said, "this ain't somethin' lots of gals would do."

"I know . . . oh . . ."

She took more of him into her mouth, suckled him like a candy stick, then released him again, this time with an audible pop.

"I mean, a lot of old-fashioned girls," she said. "They'd think this was something that was . . . you know, whorish."

"Nothing whorish about it as far as I can tell."

"I don't think my momma would be doin' this to you if she was here."

She slid her fingers up and down his erection, slick from her saliva, then swooped down again and took him in her mouth. This time she sucked him for a while, pumping him a bit with her right hand at the same time, cradling his testicles in her left.

"Um," she said, releasing him and sounding out of breath.

"Jesus, Violet," he said, "get up here . . ."

"Yes, sir."

She mounted him, reached between them to hold his cock while she slid down on it.

"Oooh," she said, "God, it feels like you're up here." She touched herself between her breasts.

Violet started bouncing up and down on him then, her breasts barely moving because they were so small and hard. He was mesmerized by her nipples, though, and reached up to touch them, flick them with his thumbs while she continued to ride him. She bit her lips, moaned, quickened her pace, and there were a couple of times when Clint thought she was going to finish but she just kept on going . . . and going . . . and going . . .

FOURTEEN

By morning Violet was sleeping soundly. Clint rose, got cleaned up, and dressed without waking her. He hoped she wouldn't have a lot of explaining to do to her mother when she got home.

He didn't wake Violet to say good-bye because he figured he'd be accompanying Bass Reeves back here with the black cowboys in tow—hopefully with them alive . . . mostly.

He went downstairs and told the desk clerk he wouldn't be around for a while, but not to check him out of his room until tomorrow.

"You want to pay for it for today even though it's empty?" the man asked.

"Exactly."

The clerk shrugged and said, "Suit yerself."

Clint picked up his rifle and saddlebags and carried them out the front door, heading for the livery stable. When he got there, Bass Reeves was already saddling his horse.

"You look a mite peaked," Reeves said to him.

"I'm fine."

Clint took Eclipse out of his stall and started to saddle him.

"That's some animal," Reeves said. "What happened to that big black you used ta have?"

"It has been a while since we saw each other," Clint said. "I had to turn Duke out to pasture."

"Looks like you got yourself a likely replacement."

Reeves's horse looked like a seven- or eight-year-old steeldust.

"Solid-looking animal yourself," Clint said.

"It'll do."

With both horses saddled, they walked their mounts outside and climbed aboard. Reeves had a canvas sack tied to his saddle horn. Clint assumed that was the sum total of their supplies.

"You get any other ideas about where to look?" Clint asked.

"Just south of the Red River," Reeves said. "We'll start at Sherman."

"Lead the way, then," Clint said. "This is your party."

"Ain't gon' be much fun for a party," Reeves muttered.

George Washington walked to the door of the lean-to he shared with his wife and two children. There were other buildings, larger ones where other families shared quarters, but they were no sturdier. A stiff wind and all they'd have would be a collection of old timber.

His wife, Wanda, came up behind him and put her arms around him.

"It's gon' be okay, George," she said.

"Yeah?" George asked. "How you know that, Wanda?"

"Because my husband, he tells me so," she said, "and he don't never lie to me."

George laughed, put his hand over his wife's.

"You got yourself a rare man if he don't never lie to you, girl."

"Oh, he's a rare one, awright." She hugged him tightly.

George looked over at their babies, a four-year-old boy and a two-year-old girl. He knew for a fact that none of the white ranch hands had children, and yet the ones they let go were all the black men with mouths to feed.

"You gon' stay awhile this time, George?" she asked.

"Can't," he said. "We didn't come back with enough food nor clothes," he explained. "We got to go out again."

"Everytime you go my heart sinks," she told him. "I feels like I'll never see you again."

"Hey, girl," he said, rubbing her arm, "remember, you said you was married to a rare man."

"A bullet can kill a rare man just as easy as a common one."

"You hush," he said. "I got to go talk to the boys."

"I'll have supper ready fo' you when you gets back," she promised.

He turned and took her in his arms.

"Got me a rare kinda woman, too, don' I?" he asked.

She smiled and said, "You sure do, George Washington."

He kissed her, grabbed his hat, and left the lean-to. He walked over to a little line shack that housed two families at the same time and knocked on the door. Both Adam Lee and Ben Jones came to the door.

"Good," Lee said. "You here."

"It's gon' be supper time soon, Adam Lee," a woman's voice called from inside.

"We'll be right back, Leona," he promised, and both he and Jones stepped outside.

"Wan' talk to you two boys special," Lee told George and Jones. "We gots to find a bigger job ta pull. Dese little ones ain't helpin' us for very long."

"What kinda bigger job you talkin' about, Adam?" George asked.

"I think you know already, George."

"That's crazy," George said.

"What's crazy about it?" Jones demanded.

"The bank in Sherman?" George Washington asked. "Come on. There's law there, they'll cut us to ribbons."

"Not if'n we figure it out right," Lee said. "And not if'n we get the right kinda help."

"What kinda help you talkin' about, Adam."

Adam Lee smiled broadly and said, "We gon' get help from Bass Reeves, hisself."

"Now dat's real crazy," George said.

"No, it ain't," Lee said. "We know he gon' be comin' for us. Well, if we's ready we can take him and make him help us."

"Bass Reeves," George Washington said, "has been a lawdog for a lot o' years, Adam. We're just cowboys with guns."

"Dat may be," Lee said, "but we gon' do it, and here's how . . ."

FIFTEEN

They camped that night in a clearing that would be easily defensible if the need arose. True, it was out in the open, but it would be that much harder for someone to creep up on them.

"You think these cowboys know you're coming for them?" Clint asked, sitting across from Reeves.

"If they smart," he said, "who else would be comin' after them?"

"Some white lawmen."

Reeves shook his head.

"This makes sense," he said.

"How do you feel about tracking down your own people?" Clint asked.

"They's outlaws," Reeves said. "They ain't my people. How do you feel when you got to track down a white man?"

"I see your point," Clint said. "I never think about the color of a man's skin if I'm going up against him."

"And I got to do the same."

They made a meal of beans and coffee, then set their watches, with Reeves first on lookout and Clint second.

"With six of them, and their families," Clint said, before turning in, "they've got to have a good-sized camp somewhere."

"That's what I'm figurin'," Reeves said, "that somebody's seen 'em, or seen some black folks—women, kids, maybe even shoppin' in some town. They got to get supplies from somewhere, I mean, other than what they stealin'."

"That's good thinking," Clint said. "I guess I'll turn in."

"I'll wake you in four hours."

Clint nodded and rolled himself up in a blanket.

George Washington ate the meager supper his wife had prepared for him and his children and cursed himself. The meal wouldn't be meager if he provided better for his family.

"What crazy scheme dat Adam Lee got for you now?" Wanda asked.

"It don't concern you," he said.

"Like hell it don't," she said. "You my husband. Everything you do concerns me, and dese babies, here."

Finally, he told her about the bank in Sherman.

"And just who he want to go into that bank?" she demanded.

"He's goin' in, and he wants me to go."

"Sure, he do," she said, "dat's because you ain't as mushmouthed as most of dese niggers is. You talks better than dem and you talks better den me." She put her fist to her mouth. "You coulda been somethin', George, if'n you didn't hook up wit' me."

"Don't you never say nothin' like that again, Wanda," he scolded her. "I ain't nothin' without you and those babies, you hear?"

He reached out his hand and she took it.

"I hear you, George."

They went back to their meal and she asked, "When you goin' to this bank?"

"Coupla days, I think," he said. "Somebody got to go to town and look it over first."

"Not you," she said, suddenly frightened again.

"No, not me," he said. "We don't want anybody seein' us until we go into that bank."

"Who then?"

"Adam say he's got somebody," George said. "A white man."

"Why would a white man help you rob a bank?"

"For a share, Wanda," George said. "Everybody does somethin' for a share."

SIXTEEN

Bass Reeves and Clint Adams rode into Sherman, Texas, the next day. Sherman was not as large as Paris, so a black man with a badge attracted even more attention there, even though Reeves had been there a few times before.

"Local sheriff's not the stupid white cracker most of them are," he told Clint. "Fella named Burton."

They rode up to the sheriff's office, dismounted, and stepped up onto the boardwalk in front of the door, which abruptly opened.

"Bass Reeves," Sheriff Tom Burton said. "Saw you ride up through my window. Come on in."

"Thank you kindly, Sheriff."

Clint followed the two men into the office.

"Sheriff, this here's a friend of mine, Clint Adams," Reeves said when they were inside.

"Adams," Burton said. "I know your rep. Glad to meet you." The two men shook hands.

Burton was a big barrel-chested man in his forties who looked like he was born with a star on his chest.

"What brings you to Sherman?" he asked.

"Lookin' for some folks been robbin' stages and travelers," Reeves said. "Maybe even a bank or two."

"We talkin' about that gang of black cowboys been tearin' the countryside up?"

"That's them."

"So the judge stuck you with trackin' them down, huh?" the other lawman asked.

"I ain't stuck," Reeves said. "Job's gotta be done."

Burton looked at Clint.

"I tell you, Adams, black, white, or blue, this man is about the best lawman I ever saw."

"That's kind of you to say, suh."

"Ain't no bull in that, Bass," Burton said. "What do you need from me?"

"Just if you seen any black folks in town, maybe buyin' some supplies?"

"Well, we got some black folks in town, but I ain't seen any strangers. You figure maybe the gang is sendin' their womenfolk into town to stock up?"

"Could be."

"I guess you'd better check over at the general store, then," Burton said. "Talk to Frank Allen. He owns it, and he can tell you who's been shoppin' there lately."

"Much obliged."

"You want me to come with you?"

"I think I can handle askin' a few questions, Sheriff," Reeves said.

"You have any trouble with any of the people in town, you let me know," Burton said. "I don't care what color your skin is, they'd better respect that badge you're wearin'."

"Yes, suh," Reeves said. "I'll let you know."

"Ah, they'll answer your questions okay," Burton added.

"You got the Gunsmith with you. Lemme walk out with you."

The three men went outside and Burton made a show of slapping Bass Reeves on the back.

"Think you'll be stayin' overnight?"

"I guess that depends on how many questions we got to ask," Reeves said.

"Well, I know we've got a couple of strangers in town, but they're two white fellas who rode in a little before you did."

"Thanks for your help, Sheriff," Clint said.

He and Reeves untied their horses and walked away leading them.

"That fella sure is in a rush to be helpful," Clint said.

"He always is," Reeves said. "I think he's one of them white folks who feel guilty, you know?"

"I know," Clint said, "but it comes off as being too . . . too much, you know?"

"I know," Reeves said. "You wanna get a beer before we ask some more questions?"

"Sounds good to me."

"There's a little saloon down the street I usually go in when I'm here that don't mind serving black folks."

"Let's go."

Reeves led the way and they tied their horses off again, this time in front of the saloon.

They entered the saloon, which was almost small enough for a man to reach out and touch two walls. Didn't have much clientele either, which suited Clint.

They walked to the small bar and the bartender looked at them.

"Howdy, Deputy," he said. "What'll ya have?"

"Two beers," Reeves said.

"Comin' up."

The bartender seemed nervous, making Clint wonder if Reeves and the man had some history he didn't know about—or didn't want to know about.

The bartender gave them each a beer, then said, "Aw, that's on the house, Deputy," when Reeves tried to pay.

"That's okay," Reeves said. "I always like to pay."

"Well, okay," the bartender said, "suit yourself."

A couple of men walked in, saw Reeves and Clint standing at the bar, and moved to the other end. They ordered drinks, didn't cast any more looks their way.

"Did you say they don't mind serving you," Clint asked, "or that they're afraid of you here?"

Reeves frowned and thought a moment.

"Seems to me I did take a couple of fellas in from here a few months ago."

"Dead or alive?"

"Dead," he said. "They called it. Drew down on me right here at the bar."

"Maybe that explains it, then," Clint said.

"You mean, that's why he's always tryin' ta give me free beer?"

"That's why."

Reeves was quiet for a moment, then shook his head and said, "Sometimes I'm a fool."

"Bass—"

"You finish your beer, Clint," the deputy said. "I'll wait for you outside."

Reeves left and Clint knew this was another one of those times he should have kept his mouth shut.

SEVENTEEN

When Clint came outside, leaving his own beer unfinished, he tried to apologize for making Reeves feel like a fool, but the lawman waved the apology away.

"Let's just get to what we come here for," he said.

They walked down the street to the general store and entered. The clerk behind the counter gave Reeves a nervous look until he saw the badge he was wearing.

"What can I do for you, Deputy?" he asked.

"Sheriff sent me over to talk to Mr. Allen," Reeves told the young man.

"Oh, sure, I'll . . . he's in the back room. I'll just go get him."

"Much obliged."

Clint looked around the store while Reeves just stood at the counter and waited.

"Pretty nicely stocked store for a small town," he said aloud.

"Thank you," Frank Allen said, coming up behind the

counter. "I try to be sure we have everything a body could need."

"Seems like you do a good job of it," Clint said.

Allen smiled, then asked Clint, "I understand you wanted to see me? The sheriff sent you over?"

"Not me," Clint said. "Him." He pointed at Bass Reeves.

"Oh." Allen looked at Reeves. "What can I do for you, Marshal?"

"Just some information, if you can," Reeves said. He asked him about any black folks coming in to stock up on supplies.

"No, no," Allen said, frowning. "We do have some black people in—real nice folks, too—but nobody who bought a lot of supplies."

"I'd be interested in strangers," Reeves said. "Folks you ain't never seen before?"

"Well, I can't say as we've had any strangers in here lately—"

"There was those fellas in here today, Mr. Allen," the young clerk said. "They was strangers I never seen before."

Allen gave the boy a look, then said to Reeves, "But those were white men."

"I see," Reeves said. "Well, thank ya kindly for your co-operation."

"Anytime," Allen said. "Always ready to help the law."

Clint and Reeves stepped outside.

"What are you thinking?" Clint asked.

"He ain't the kind would lie for black people," Reeves said, "so I believe him."

"He didn't want that young clerk talking to us," Clint said.

"I noticed that," Reeves said. "Prolly because the two strangers in town are white."

"Who says white men and black men can't work together?" Clint asked.

Reeves looked at him and said, "Not me."

Arch Wilson and Denny Radke entered the bank together. Radke stayed by the front window while Wilson went to the teller's window to inquire about opening an account. He kept the clerk talking long enough for Radke to study the interior of the bank. When Radke cleared his throat, Wilson thanked the clerk and the two men left.

Outside, Radke said, "This is what we've fallen to? Casin' a bank for a bunch of niggers?"

"Denny, Denny," Wilson said, "relax. The niggers take the bank, and we take the niggers. It's gonna be as easy as that. You saw that place in there? Even a bunch of niggers can rob that bank."

"Why don't we just take it ourselves?" Radke said. "We could do it right now, you and me."

"This town's got law, and while the law is lookin' for a bunch of nigger bank robbers, we'll be goin' to Mexico with the cash."

"Okay," Radke said, "okay, you're makin' the decisions—for now."

"Don't worry, Denny," Wilson said. "I ain't never taken you down the wrong trail yet, have I?"

"Maybe not," Radke said, "but we ain't rich yet neither, are we?"

"No, we ain't," Wilson said, "yet. But we will be, real soon."

"Yeah, if them niggers can take this bank without trippin' over each other."

"Oh, they'll take it," Wilson said, "even if we have to teach them how."

EIGHTEEN

Bass Reeves and Clint went looking for the two white strangers in town, but never found them. Apparently, they had not checked into a hotel. They rode in and rode out.

"So what were they doing in town?" Clint wondered aloud.

"Don't know," Reeves said, "but it prolly has nothin' ta do with us."

They had stopped in a small café and when the waitress didn't give Reeves a funny or cross look, they sat down and ordered. The food wasn't very good, but they were hungry, so it would do.

"Tell me more about this Sheriff Burton," Clint said.

"What's ta tell?"

"Does he always treat you like that?"

"Every time," Reeves said. "He goes out of his way to respect the badge."

"But that stuff about you being the best lawman he knew?"

"He don't mean that."

"Maybe he does."

Clint was trying to make up for what he'd said in the saloon, making Reeves realize that he wasn't respected there, just feared.

"Don't worry about it, Clint," Reeves said. "I don't think much of him as a lawman, so I don't much care what he thinks of me."

"You are a hell of a lawman, Bass," Clint said. "You know that, don't you?"

"I reckon I'm okay," Reeves said, "but it sure means a whole lot more comin' from you. I'm obliged."

"Just know that *I* mean it."

Reeves held up a big hand and said, "I will, if you stop tryin' ta convince me."

"Okay," Clint said. "Point taken."

They finished their food, leaving the rest of the bad coffee, and decided to wash their meal down with a beer. They found a small saloon that Reeves had never been in before and entered. As usual, they attracted stares but the badge on Reeves's shirt convinced the men to look away.

"Two beers," Clint told the bartender.

"Sure thing, Deputies," he said.

He brought them and Clint paid.

"Next move?" Clint asked.

"They hit a stage not too far from here about a week ago," Reeves said. "We might as well ride over there and then start searching in a . . . whadaya call it?" Reeves made circles with his finger.

"A search pattern?"

"That's it," Reeves said, "that's the word I was lookin' for."

"Okay," Clint said. "I can go along with that."

"And any towns we pass we can check in and see if they remember any black folks buying supplies."

"Tell me about the judge," Clint said.

"What about him?"

"How does he compare to Parker?"

"He's about he same," Reeves said, "'cept he don't hang so many."

"Nobody hung as many as Hanging Judge Parker," Clint observed.

"They was usually murderers, though."

Clint didn't comment. He'd had his own run-ins with Judge Parker, and since he'd never worked for the man, he did not have any fond memories of their encounters.

They finished their beer and Reeves said, "I figure we should be headin' out, and camp like we did last night. No point in gettin' comfortable in a hotel bed."

"Suits me," Clint said. "I think I've seen all I want to of this town."

They walked outside, mounted their horses, and rode out without any further discussion.

NINETEEN

Adam Lee and George Washington were waiting at a pre-arranged location for the two white men, Wilson and Radke.

"I don't trust these white men," George said.

"Hell, George," Lee said, "I don't trust any white man, but we couldn't go inta town and look that bank over our ownselves, could we?"

"No," George said, "but you know they'll try and take the money off us after we get it."

Adam Lee chuckled.

"Oh, I knowed dat from the time I first met dem boys," he said. "Don't you worry, we'll be ready for 'em."

"Here they come," George said.

They watched as the two white men rode toward them at a leisurely pace, in no hurry at all. Lee folded his arms. He was the leader of the black cowboys, but even he knew that George was the smarter one, the one who talked better and was more educated. But that didn't mean he was going to let him be the leader. Because as smart as he thought George was, Lee didn't think George had what it took to be a strong leader.

Together, though, they made a great one.

The white men finally reached them and dismounted.

"Anybody got a bottle of whiskey?" Denny Radke asked.

"We didn't bring no whiskey," Adam Lee said.

Radke laughed and pulled a full bottle out of his saddlebags.

"We didn't come here to drink whiskey," George said.

"Hello, George," Arch Wilson said. "Denny and me wouldn't dream of sharin' a bottle with you two niggers. Naw, this is yours to take back with ya."

He handed the bottle to Lee, who accepted it. Sometimes George was frustrated with Adam Lee, because he didn't think the man knew when he was being insulted or made fun of.

"Thank ya kindly, then," he said. "Did you fellas see the bank?"

"Oh, we saw it all right," Wilson said. "It's a cracker box. You fellas won't have a lick of trouble with it . . . if you do it right."

"Whatcha mean, do it right?" Lee asked.

"Well," Denny Radke said, "you can't just walk into a bank, take out your guns, and say, 'This is a stickup.' "

"We can't?" Lee asked.

"No, ya can't," Wilson said.

"You fellas have robbed banks before?" George asked.

"Lots of 'em," Radke said.

"So then you could tell us how to do it," Lee said.

"We could," Wilson said, scratching the stubble on his chin, "we could do that, couldn't we, Arch?"

"Yeah, we could do that," Wilson said. "'Course, we'd need to get a taste . . ."

"A taste?" Lee asked.

"They want to be paid," George said.

"We are payin' dem," Adam Lee said.

"More," George said, "Adam, they want to be paid more."

"Not a lot more," Wilson said.

"Just a little more," Radke said, holding his thumb and forefinger up. "Like this."

"I tell ya what," Wilson said. "Why don't we tell you what we saw, then we can discuss how much that's worth? And then we can negotiate for the rest of it? How's that sound?"

"We don't want to stay around here too long," George Washington said.

"It won't take long, George," Wilson promised. "It won't take long a'tall."

It took half an hour for the white men to wheedle the promise of more money out of the two black men, and then they mounted up and rode away with the promise to meet in that same place in three day's time.

"You really think they're gonna be there in three days?" Radke asked.

"They're a proud bunch of people, those niggers," Wilson said. "I think if they said they're gonna be there, they're gonna be there."

"So we're gonna trust 'em?"

"Hell, no," Wilson said. "We're gonna follow 'em."

"We just got us a lesson in bank robbin'," Adam Lee said.

"Yeah, well, if they so good at it, why they not rich, huh?" George asked.

"Never you mind," Lee said. "We's the one gon' be rich, and soon."

He slapped George on the back and the two men mounted up and rode off.

TWENTY

Reeves and Clint arrived at the point in the road where the stage had been hit.

"It turned over here," Reeves said, pointing to the ground.

"They must have had to chase it, and it didn't make this curve," Clint said. "What are we, ten, twelve miles from Sherman?"

"About that."

"How many people on the stage?"

"Four."

"Anybody hurt?"

Reeves looked at him.

"Two hurt, two dead—one of them a woman."

"Jesus," Clint said. "So we're hunting these fellas down for murder?"

Reeves nodded.

"That make a difference?"

"Some," Clint said. "It makes a difference in how much sympathy I'm willing to feel for them."

"Let's ride back a ways," Reeves said, "see if we can find the spot where they picked the stage up."

"And maybe even find the spot where they were waiting," Clint said.

About ten minutes later they thought they'd found the spot where the gang had likely picked the stage up.

"Lots of traffic on this road since last week," Reeves said, "but it looks like the stage mighta picked up speed here."

"If those wheel ruts are from the stage," Clint said.

There were bluffs on both sides, so they split up to see if they could find the place where the renegade cowboys had been hiding and waiting . . .

Reeves fired a shot, so Clint stopped looking and rode over to the bluff on the other side, where Reeves was waiting for him.

"Over here," the lawman said. "Not so much traffic here. Tracks are still clear."

Reeves led Clint on foot behind some brush.

"They had a view from behind here," Reeves said, pointing down.

Clint looked down, saw prints from horses and from men. Looked like a jumble to him, but Reeves could read them with his tracker's eye.

"Six horses, six men," he said.

"Can we track these prints?" Clint asked.

"We prolly could if they went right from here to their hideout, but they didn't. They chased that stage, picked it clean when it turned over, and left those folks to die, which two of 'em did."

"Anything distinctive about any of these horse prints?" Clint asked.

"Only one," Reeves said, pointing. "It's unshod."

"They wouldn't leave a cow pony unshod, unless . . ." Clint said.

"Unless it ain't a cow pony," Reeves said. "It's prolly an Indian pony."

"That shouldn't be too hard to track."

"If we can pick it up again back where the stage turned over," Reeves said.

"Only one way to find out," Clint said.

They mounted their horses again and retraced their steps to where the stage came to a stop.

They walked it, leaving their horses a ways away so they wouldn't confuse the issue. But there were enough other tracks to confuse it anyway. In the end, Clint had to stop looking and leave it to Reeves.

"So who was the woman who was killed?" he asked.

"Hmm?" Reeves was busily studying the ground.

"The woman in the stage," Clint said. "You said a woman was killed."

"Oh," he said, "somebody's wife. They was comin' ta town to get settled, I think."

"A white woman?"

"There was only whites in the stage," Reeves said.

"And what's her husband doing now?"

"I don't know."

"Do we know where he is?"

"No."

"Well, is he still in town?"

Reeves looked at Clint.

"I ain't asked. Why?"

"I'm just wondering, is all," Clint said. "I'm wondering why there's no posse out after these jaspers."

"Because we're after 'em."

"What about other jobs they pulled?" Clint asked. "Other towns? Nobody's ever sent a posse after them?"

Reeves thought about it, then admitted, "I ain't asked."

"Well," Clint said, "next time we're in town, maybe out of curiosity, I'll ask, if you don't mind."

"Hell," Reeves said, "I don't mind."

With that, he gave his attention back over to the ground.

TWENTY-ONE

"You can't trust white men."

It really didn't matter who said this. All six men and their families—except their children—were gathered together outside their "homes" to discuss their next job. The children were inside the largest building with one of the older women to watch over them.

They all looked at Wanda Washington, who had spoken those words—this time. It wasn't like they hadn't heard them before.

"And you 'specially can't trust these white men," she said. "They's outlaws."

"Wanda," Adam Lee said, "we's outlaws, too."

"We's tryin' ta feed our kids," Wanda shot back at him. "They's jus' greedy men."

"Yeah, dey are," Lee said, "but we needed dem to look at the bank fo' us."

"No, we don't need dem no mo'," Ben Jones said.

"No, we don't," Lee said, "but we owes dem money."

"Is dey gon' settle for what we owes dem?" Jones asked. "Or is dey gon' try ta take it all."

"Oh," George Washington said, "they're gonna try to take it all. We knows that."

"So den we's gon' have ta kill 'em," Jones said.

"Maybe," Lee said, "but ain't no point talkin' 'bout dat now. What we got to figure out now is who's goin' into town and when."

"What about dat lawman in Sherman?" Wanda asked. "What we know 'bout him?"

"He been wearin' dat badge o' his fo' a long time," Ben Jones said. "But he ain't no good at it no mo'. He be lazy."

"Any deputies?" Leona Lee asked.

"Not a one," Ben Jones said.

"Accordin' ta those white men, you mean," Leona said.

Of all the women, Leona was probably the most educated and well-spoken. She was also a beauty. Whenever they were gathered together like this, George Washington found it hard to keep his eyes off her—something he tried desperately to keep from his own wife. But Leona had smooth, ebony skin, large, well-shaped breasts under her plain dress, and did not show the effects of childbirth that some of the other wives showed. Her hips and thighs had not gotten heavier, nor had her arms and legs, and the other wives often talked about her behind her back. George thought it was unfair of them to dislike her because she was beautiful and her big nipples were always showing through her clothes.

She was too good, he thought, for Adam Lee, who was a simple man with no education. The only thing he had going for him was that he could get men worked up to follow him. It was his idea for them to go out on their own after they all got laid off—hit the outlaw trail—but Lee wouldn't do it without George. He needed George's brain, and his ability to blend in with white people, who sometimes accepted him because he was light-skinned, and he talked like them.

But George knew the great danger here was that he was falling in love—or lust—with another man's wife. And worse, she knew it. He could tell by the way she looked back at him.

"Well, yeah, accordin' ta dem," her husband said.

"Seems to me we better at least send one man into town to look for ourselves."

That said, she looked right at George.

"Why you lookin' at my husband, Leona Lee?" Wanda demanded, placing her hands on her ample hips.

"Because he's the only one who won't stand out," Leona said.

"Well, you talks pretty good," Wanda said. "Maybe you should go inta town."

"Okay, okay," George said, "none of the women are goin' into town. Right, Adam?"

"That's right," Lee said.

"So I guess that just leaves me," George said.

"If'n you'll do it, George," Lee said. "We just need to be sure before we go ridin' in there."

"I guess I could go in and just look around, listen to folks talk."

Wanda was fuming. Her hands were still on her hips and she was glaring at Leona, who was pretending not to notice. Wanda's fists were formidable, her fingers thick and blunt, unlike Leona's lovely, tapered ones. George was ready to jump in and save Leona if Wanda decided to commence whaling on her.

"Okay, den," Lee said, "we cain't do nothin' until George goes ta town and comes back."

"That gon' be days," Ben Jones said. "We gots ta feed dese here babies."

"We can take care of that," Lee said. "Dere's a small tradin' post about twenty miles from here. Take us only a day ta go there, get some supplies, and come back."

"We ain't doin' so good on money, either," Jones said.

"I didn't say nothin' about buyin' no supplies," Lee said. "Now, did I?"

TWENTY-TWO

Denny Radke and Arch Wilson were in a small town called Rector, about ten miles east of Sherman. They didn't want to be anywhere near Sherman when those black cowboys robbed the bank.

Radke had picked the town because there was a gal in the whorehouse there that he liked. She was a big girl, not fat, but solid, with big meaty breasts and rump. Her name was Anna. The girls in the house called her Big Fat Anna, but oddly enough she was one of the more popular girls there. That fact drove a lot of the prettier, skinnier girls crazy. They couldn't figure out what it was she had that made her so popular, because it just never occurred to them that it could be the extra weight, the meat on her bones.

Radke liked her for two reasons. One, she sucked his dick, which a lot of the other girls wouldn't do. This gal, however, took to it like a mule to a salt lick. She was sucking him now, making loud, slurping noises as her head bobbed up and down. He was holding her head lightly, lifting his hips up off the bed as she sucked him, crouched down between his legs. In that position, he could see her fat ass sticking up and it was starting to get him too excited.

"Slow down, gal," he said, trying to pull her off him, "I don't wanna finish up just yet."

Reluctantly, she let him slide wetly out of her mouth and looked up at him with a big smile. She wasn't a pretty girl, but when he was with her he didn't spend a lot of time looking at her plain face. He either watched the top of her head bob up and down, or he was looking at her from behind.

That was the other thing about her he liked. She didn't mind getting down on all fours for a man, although he really didn't want to stick it in her ass. He was afraid he might get his peter stuck between those two mountainous buttocks. No, he liked to slide it up between her thighs and into her squishy pussy, and then he liked to smack her while he fucked her.

She didn't mind.

They moved around on the bed so she could get on all fours. Lucky for him he had a long, skinny dick and could slide up between those fat thighs and into her. He started fucking her like that and every once in a while he'd haul off a smack on her ass. He knew he wasn't hurting her, but she'd squeal anyway. On her hands and knees like that, not only her tits hung down and swayed, but her belly did, too. He pulled her up onto her knees, and as she twisted to look at him over her shoulder he reached out and slapped one of her tits. They were so meaty and solid, it was just like smacking her on the ass. Same sound.

He was enjoying the hell out of himself.

Arch Wilson had different tastes.

The girl he was with a few doors down was a petite blonde with no tits and an ass like a boy. She had a face like an angel, though, and he liked fucking her while looking down at her sweet face, so it was always the same for them: missionary position.

The girl's name was Melanie, and she didn't mind being with Wilson, because he never asked her to do anything weird or unusual. He'd just ride her like that and stare at her face the whole time.

Fucking this girl was perfect for an outlaw like Wilson, who never had a kind thought for anyone. He actually felt like he was fucking an angel, and for a bad man like him that was a mighty good feeling.

After they finished with their women, they went down to the parlor and left the whorehouse.

"Don't know how you can stick yer dick in that fat cow," Wilson complained.

"You oughtta try it some time," Radke said. "All that extra meat—especially in the winter. It's mighty warmin'. And those huge tits? They got the biggest nipples. Tell ya what, I don't know how you can be with that skinny gal. I'd break her in half the first time."

"She's got a face like an angel."

"Yeah, well, does she let ya stick it in her face? That would be somethin'."

"Naw, she don't do that," Wilson said.

"Well, does she let ya kiss 'er?"

"Yeah, that she does," Wilson said, "but I don't wanna kiss her, I just wanna lay into her, ya know?"

"Yeah, I know it," Radke said. "That's how I feel about Big Fat Anna. I don't even wanna see her face."

"Can't blame you for that," Wilson said. "That sure ain't a pretty gal."

"Yeah, but that big ass," Radke said, "that's a pretty sight, especially when it's red from me smackin' it."

"You're a sick man, Denny," Wilson said. "Come on, let's get somethin' ta eat."

In a small saloon that served food, they ate some stew and drank some beer and talked about the black cowboys.

"You really think those niggers are gonna be able to take that bank?" Radke asked.

"Why not? The one thing we told 'em that was true was that the bank is a cracker box. Anybody could rob that place."

"And then we take the money from them."

"It's a simple plan," Wilson said. "If they don't get it done, if they're stupid enough to get caught doin' it, it's no skin off our noses. We just go look for somethin' else, and we didn't take no risks."

"So what are we gonna do, just wait around here until we hear it was done?"

"We're supposed to meet them in that same spot in three days," Wilson said, "and that's just what we're gonna do."

"Suits me," Radke said. "That's three days of stickin' my dick in Fat Anna and slappin' her ass and tits."

Wilson studied his partner for a moment, then said, "Yeah, you're a sick, sick man."

TWENTY-THREE

Eventually, Reeves was able to dig out the track of the unshod horse from among all the others scattered in the ground.

"There it is," he said, pointing.

Clint stared for a long time, but it was no use. He couldn't see anything.

"I'll have to take your word for it," he said finally.

"Oh, it's there," Reeves said.

"Then the question is, can we now follow it?" Clint asked.

Reeves continued to stare at the ground with his hands on his hips.

"It's gonna be tough, and slow goin'," he said, "but we can try." Reeves looked at Clint.

"Hey, so let's try," Clint said. "I'll just stay behind you and out of trouble."

"Even if it don't lead us all the way," Reeves said, "maybe it'll give us a direction."

"Which is more than we've got now," Clint said.

• • •

George Washington rode into Sherman, Texas, determined
not to speak to anyone unless he had to. He figured even if
someone was looking for them they'd be looking for more
than just one lone black man—and an unarmed man, at that.
He'd decided not to wear a gun, because what kind of outlaw
doesn't wear a gun? And from the wear of his clothes, people would probably figure him for a workingman—farm,
ranch, store, whatever.

He reined his horse in and dismounted, careful to stay
away from the center of town. All he wanted to do was
walk around and keep his ears open and get the information he needed. An hour or two, then he'd get the hell out of
there.

Reeves reined in again—third time in ten minutes—and
leaned down, his head along his horse's neck. He hadn't
been kidding. This was slow work, all right, but Clint just
kept quiet and followed along. Once again Reeves sat up
straight in the saddle and off they went again.

Leona Lee was waiting impatiently a mile from the camp.
She'd picked the spot very carefully, because there was a
stand of trees off to the right with a clearing right in the
center. From the road no one could see what was going on,
and that was what she wanted.

Her heart was beating quickly and her hands were
sweating. Looking down at herself, she could see her own
nipples pushing out against the fabric of the threadbare
dress she was wearing. She pressed her hands against her
body and flattened the dress down even more. She knew
she looked better than all the other women in camp, and
that all the men noticed. She liked it.

What she didn't like was that her husband didn't seem to notice. He didn't notice when it was time to eat, and he didn't notice that the other men looked at her. And he didn't touch her, ever, not since the birth of their second child. He seemed to have lost interest in sex altogether, to the point where she wasn't even worried that he might be seeing other women. She didn't think any woman would interest him—especially not since they had all banded together under his leadership.

So now she was going to take advantage of the fact that the other men looked at her, wanted her, and she was going to take the one she wanted.

If he'd have her.

TWENTY-FOUR

George had accomplished what he'd set out to do. He'd learned what he had gone to town to learn, had managed not to speak to anyone, and had gone virtually unnoticed. He'd achieved this in spite of the fact that he was black. Probably he'd seemed nonthreatening—he carried no gun, wore no badge, asked nothing of anyone.

Now he was riding back to the camp—he could not bring himself to call it a hideout—and saw someone standing in the road ahead of him. It was a woman, and his stomach did a flip-flop when he realized who it was. There was only one woman in camp shaped like that.

As he reached her, she stood with her legs apart, hands on her hips, proud body on display.

"I been waiting for you, George Washington."

"Why?" he asked. "What's wrong? Where's Adam?"

"Him and the others went to the trading post for supplies," she said. "They'll be back tonight."

"Where are your babies?"

"They're fine," she said. "They're bein' looked after."

"Then what are you doin' out here?"

"Like I told you," she said. "I've been waiting for you."

Mouth dry, he asked, "Why?"

"I got something to show you."

"What?"

"Well, get down from that horse and come see," she said, "I ain't gonna bite you."

George looked around but there was no one else in sight. It was just the two of them. He dismounted.

"Come on," she said, reaching out to take his hand. As she led him, he nudged the horse toward a stand of trees. When they got to the center, there as a clearing with a blanket in the middle.

"W-what did you wanna show me?" he asked.

"That blanket." She pointed. He couldn't help but look at her body. She didn't have an ounce of fat on her, the way her dress clung to her made that clear, and yet she had those big, fine breasts and those nipples that looked like big grapes under her dress. His wife Wanda had spread out in the hips and thighs, and her breasts were starting to sag. She was a fine woman, a good wife and mother, but there was no passion between them, no fire.

He and Leona, they were about to set fire to those trees just by looking at each other.

"I see you lookin' at me, George," she said, "you and the other men."

Good Lord, he thought as she touched herself, touched her own body.

"I got a burnin' in me, George," she said, "and my husband don't care to put it out. You wanna help me put it out, George?" She leaned forward and lowered her voice. "Or you wanna help me set it free?"

"Goddamn—" he said, and reached for her.

•   •   •

"This is hopeless," Bass Reeves finally said. "I lost it."

"Can't blame you," Clint said. "The ground here isn't going to hold tracks for very long."

There was hard clay, there was grass, there was everything but what they needed to hold and retain a track.

"Well, we seem ta be headin' west," Reeves said. "What we could do is just keep goin' that way and hope for the best."

"Sounds like a plan."

"If we reach a town, we can find out what they can tell us."

"Do you know what the next town would be?"

"A little place called Rector," Reeves said. "Ain't much there but a saloon and a whorehouse. You ever heard of Big Fat Anna?"

"No."

"Supposed to be the biggest whore around." Reeves looked at Clint, smiled, and held his arms out as if he was trying to get his arms around a woman. "Biggest."

Both men laughed.

"Well, then," Clint said, "at least the town has got something to see."

"Let's head that way, then," Reeves said. "Who knows, the tracks might show up again."

"Why are you doin' this?" Seth Ripkin asked. He was being held at gunpoint by one black man while four others helped themselves to supplies. "I always treated you people good."

"Oh, yeah," Ben Jones said, sticking the barrel of the gun into the man's side, "you one of the good white people."

"Okay," Adam Lee said, "we got what we come for."

The four men mounted up. Then one of them produced

a gun and pointed it at Ripkin while Ben Jones got on his horse.

"You send anybody after us, you gon' be dead," Adam Lee told him.

"Who do I got to send?" Ripkin asked. "I'm here alone, and now you ruined me."

"Oh, yeah, you ruined," Lee said. "You try livin' like us and see if you ruined, white man."

"You people," Ripkin said, "you're no better than savages. You're as bad as the red man."

The remark incensed Lee for some reason, and he drew his gun and shot Ripkin through the chest.

"What'd ya go and do that for, Adam?" Jones asked. "Now they gon' be after us for murder."

"Wrong, Ben," Lee said, holstering his gun, "they ain't gon' be after us at all. They ain't even gon' know we was here."

He turned his horse and rode off, the other men following him. Only Ben Jones remained, looking down at the white man who had never done them any harm. Maybe he deserved to be robbed just because he was white, but he didn't deserve to be killed.

TWENTY-FIVE

Leona was hot—physically hot. Her skin seemed to burn George, even through her dress. He kissed her, their mouths coming together in a searing embrace, and then she backed away from him and pulled the dress over her head. Her breasts, large and rounded, were tipped with big chocolate brown nipples. George had always wondered about those nipples, so he wasted no time. He took her big breasts in his hands, squeezed them, and brought them to his mouth. She caught her breath as he sucked her nipples, and she slid her hand between their bodies to cup his crotch, since he was generating some heat of his own.

Impatiently, she undid his belt and pulled his trousers down around his ankles. She fell to her knees, grabbed his rigid penis and rubbed it all over her face. He bent his knees slightly and grabbed her head as she took him into her mouth and began to suck him wetly, avidly, her hands digging into his muscular buttocks. He couldn't believe he was doing this, that he was in Leona's mouth, that he

was touching her, possessing her and—moments later—
that he was inside of her while she lay on her back on the
blanket. It was wrong, he knew, a betrayal of her husband,
his friend, his wife, and yet there was no way he could
stop.

And no way he wanted to.

Clint and Bass Reeves rode into Rector, Texas, late in the
day. People gave them looks, of course. This town was even
smaller than Sherman. Clint started to wonder how Bass
Reeves—and other black men—could do it, live each day
under this scrutiny. And then he realized how much he had
in common with the black man, for he lived under constant
scrutiny every day of his life as well.

"Any law here?" he asked Reeves.

"None to mention," Reeves said. "Technically, the sheriff from Sherman has jurisdiction when the need for a lawman comes up."

"Well, there's law here now."

Reeves looked at Clint, then realized what he meant and
nodded.

"I guess you're right."

They dismounted in front of a saloon, since there was
no sheriff's office. As they entered, they attracted the attention of the patrons, who filled only about a quarter of the
place, which was a decent-sized establishment.

They were of particular interest to two men sitting at a
table together, nursing beers.

Arch Wilson saw the black man wearing the deputy marshal's badge enter the saloon with another white man, and
nudged Radke with his boot.

"Didn't we see that big black buck in Sherman?" he asked.

Radke looked over and said, "Yeah, and that other fella, too."

"What the hell are they doing here?" Wilson wondered out loud.

"Lookin' for us, maybe?"

"Denny, we ain't done nothin' hereabouts for the law to come lookin' for us."

"Oh, yeah," Radke said. "I forgot."

"Ya know what?" Radke asked, moving his chair closer to his partner's.

"What?"

"Maybe they sent a black lawman to look for some black outlaws."

"Hey, that makes sense. You think we should warn them niggers?"

"What for? As long as the lawman's not in Sherman when they hit the bank, why should they worry?"

"So what do we do?"

"Nothin'," Wilson said, "absolutely nothin'."

George and Leona rolled around on the ground—on the blanket and off—clutching at each other, unmindful now of where they were, who might be passing, or who might be looking for them.

They came to a stop with her on top, his throbbing, rock-hard dick buried deeply inside her.

"Oh, Lord," she said, pressing her hands to his powerful chest, "I knew it would be good, but I didn't know it would be this good. I never knew it could be this good."

He reached for her breasts again, unable to get enough of them—enough of her!

No, it had never been this good with Wanda—ever—and that would make him feel even more guilty about what they were doing.

But not until later—much later.

TWENTY-SIX

"We don't belong with these people," Leona said, pulling her dress back on.

George felt sad—sad that she was covering up that amazing body, sad that they wouldn't, or shouldn't, do this again.

"What are you talking about?"

She knelt down on the blanket with him and grabbed his arm.

"We should go away together," she said, urgently.

"You're crazy, woman," he said. "We got families. We got people depending on us."

"George," she said, "you and me are better than these people. We're . . . smarter, more educated. Didn't you go to sixth grade?"

"Yeah, but—"

"Nobody else has," she said. "I went through fifth grade, but I've learned more along the way." She squeezed his arm painfully. "We belong together, and we don't belong with these people. Besides, they're all gonna get killed."

He pulled his arm away and stood up, staring down at her.

"You're evil, woman!"

"Yes," she said, "I'm bad, but so are you. Look at you. You're naked. You're still wet from me."

She reached out and stroked his heavy testicle sack, causing him to jump away from her and grab for his trousers.

"I musta been crazy doin' this with you, Leona," he said.

"Crazy *for* me," she said, getting to her knees. "Tell me you don't want to be in my mouth again. Wanda ever do that for you? I don't think so."

Damn the woman. She was right on both counts.

"Whadaya think your husband would do if he found out about this?"

"He'd make a fool move like comin' after you, and you'd kill 'im," Leona said.

"And what about your kids?"

"Adam's got a sister. She'll take 'em. See, there's nothin' keepin' us from bein' together, George."

"What about my kids?"

"They'd be with their mother. You can't resist, George. You belong to me after this."

"I got to get back," he said. "Adam and the others will be gettin' back from the tradin' post. Clean yourself up, woman, and then come on back to camp."

"Whatever you say, George," she said, "cause you're my man now."

"You got a man," he said, "and I got a woman. This can't work, Leona."

"Then why you always throwin' them hot looks my way?" she demanded. "Undressin' me with your eyes, gettin' me all hot and bothered?"

"It's got to stop, Leona," he said. "It's all got to stop."

"After this?" she asked. "After you been in my pussy and in my mouth. You want to put it in my ass, George? You can if you want to."

"Jesus," he said, not because he was appalled, but because he was suddenly fully erect again.

"Look at you," she said. "You ready again. Come on, darlin'. One more time before we go back."

She started pulling her dress up again, but he got out of there before she could bare her breasts. If he saw her breasts again, and those chocolate nipples, he knew he wouldn't be able to resist.

TWENTY-SEVEN

"We're being watched," Clint said to Bass Reeves.

"I know," Reeves said. "By everybody. I'm always bein' watched—"

"No," Clint said, "this isn't about you being black. We got two fellas real interested in us since we first walked in."

"Where?" Reeves asked without turning.

"Back behind my shoulder to the right. Use the mirror, you'll get a clear view."

"Not in that mirror," Reeves said, referring to how dirty it was, "but I seem 'em."

"Know them?"

"Never seen 'em before."

"I think it was your badge that got their attention," Clint said.

"Maybe they're wanted," Reeves said. "If they keep to themselves, I don't see no reason why we gotta be concerned."

"Maybe not," Clint said. "I'll just keep an eye on them."

• • •

"I got an idea," Wilson said.

"What?" Radke asked.

"Just follow my lead. Come on."

"Where?"

"We're gonna get another beer."

"Hey—"

But Wilson was already on his way to the bar. Radke had no choice but to follow.

Clint saw the two men approaching the bar and elbowed Reeves. They didn't appear to be posing any danger, so both men remained relaxed, leaning on the bar.

"Hey, you fellas are deputies, ain'tcha?" Wilson asked.

Rather than explain that it was only Reeves who wore a badge, Clint said, "Yup."

"See, Denny, I told ya. Hey, barkeep, two more. You fellas want another?"

"No," Reeves said, "we're good."

"Well, my friend and I were wonderin' if you fellas were looking for some, uh, black fellas."

"What kind of black fellas?" Clint asked.

"I dunno," Wilson said. "We just saw five or six black men on horseback ridin' south of here, thought it was kinda odd. You know, that many nig—black men together on horses? Then I remembered there's this gang . . . what are they called, Denny?"

"Oh, uh . . . the black cowboys, or somethin' like that?"

"That's it," Wilson said, as the bartender put down two more beers on the bar. "The black cowboys."

"What makes you think we're lookin' for them?" Clint asked.

"I dunno, just seemed to make sense to me," Wilson

said. "Ya know, send a black lawman to catch some black outlaws?"

"You saw them south of here, ya say?" Reeves asked.

"That's right," Wilson said. "And they was headin' south, too, right, Denny?"

"Right, Arch."

"I'm Arch. This is Denny," Wilson said unnecessarily.

"Well," Clint said, "we're much obliged for the information."

"Sure thing," Wilson said, picking up the two beers. "We'll just go back to our table and go on mindin' our own business now."

Reeves nodded and the two men went back to their table.

"Whadaya think?" Reeves asked.

"They were lying."

"Why?"

"I can tell when a man's lying," Clint said, "but I can't tell why. That we'll have to find out."

"That was pretty smart, Arch," Radke said as they sat back down. "Sendin' them off on a wild-goose chase, huh?"

"Just until our friendly niggers pull that bank job," Wilson said, "and until we get the money off them. After that, I don't care what happens to them."

Wilson saw Clint and Reeves push away from the bar and head for the door, tossing a glance their way first. He lifted his beer mug in a salute, and then took a drink.

"Stupid lawmen," he said.

"Yeah," Radke agreed.

TWENTY-EIGHT

Outside the saloon, Clint and Reeves walked across the street and stopped in front of a small general store.

"Why would two white men be sending us off in the wrong direction?" Clint asked.

"Because they're working with the black cowboys?" Reeves asked.

"That's the obvious answer."

"But why?" Reeves asked. "Those two don't seem like the type of fellas who'd be friends with *niggers*."

"I know," Clint said, "he did slip once or twice, trying to be careful not to use that word in front of you."

"Then, why would they be helpin' them?"

"Well, the other answer is obvious, too, isn't it?" Clint asked.

"Money."

Clint rubbed his jaw.

"They're getting ready to pull some kind of a job," Clint said, "and these two are going to share in the proceeds."

"Why don't we take them in?" Reeves asked.

"On what charge?"

"I don't need no charge," Reeves said. "Ain't no law in this town for me to have to explain it to."

"And there's no jail to hold them in," Clint said. "We'd have to take them back to Sherman—and there is a lawman there."

"What do you suggest, then?"

"Follow them, see where they take us," Clint said. "They're going to have to meet up with the gang to get paid."

"Yeah," Reeves said, "but that'll be after the job is pulled. My job is to stop them before they do it."

"So what do you suggest?"

"We keep goin' in the direction of those tracks," Reeves said. "If these two are gonna meet up with the gang, we'll see 'em again."

"That's probably true."

"Or we could split up."

"I'm out here to help you," Clint said. "Going off on my own isn't going to do that. You're the law, and the tracker."

"You tellin' me the great Gunsmith might get lost?" Reeves asked. His accompanying laugh was the first Clint had heard out of him since they had met up again.

"It just might happen," Clint admitted.

"All right," Reeves said. "At least we ain't lettin' them send us off in the wrong direction."

We hope, Clint added to himself.

"Now what do we do?" Radke asked Wilson.

"We stay put," Wilson said. "If they're suspicious of us, they'll wanna follow us."

"So we don't go nowhere."

"Right."

"And I get to go back to the whorehouse and ride Big Fat Anna some more."

Wilson made a face.

"Whatever you wanna do, Denny."

"You know," Radke said, "she really ain't that fat, just kinda . . . solid."

"Like I said, partner," Wilson said. "You can do whatever you want to do. We got three days ta kill."

Clint and Bass Reeves walked back to their horses and mounted up.

"That there's the whorehouse," Reeves said, nodding toward the building as they passed it.

"Uh-huh."

"Sure you don't wanna go in and take a look at Big Fat Anna?" Reeves asked.

"What about you?"

"She's white," Reeves said. "Wouldn't do for a black man to go with a white whore. But if I was gonna go with a white whore, it'd be one with extra meat on her bones."

"That's okay," Clint said. "I don't usually pay for my women."

"They come lookin' for you, then?"

"Sometimes they do."

For a second Clint thought Reeves might know what had happened between him and Violet back in Paris, but then the feeling passed. Reeves was chuckling.

"You a lucky man, then," he said. "I ain't never had women chasin' after me."

"That might be," Clint said, "because you've been married a long time, and you just never noticed."

TWENTY-NINE

When George got back to camp, the other men had not yet arrived. He was shaken by his encounter with Leona—shaken by the power of his own lust. He loved his babies, and he loved his wife, but a wanton woman like Leona was hard for a man to resist.

Was she right, though? Were the two of them alike, and did they not belong with the rest? George had to admit that he'd had his own thoughts about this from time to time.

As he approached the lean-to he shared with his family, Wanda came to the door and smiled as he approached. Funny, he'd always known that she had put on some pounds over the years of their marriage, but today was the first time he ever noticed that she had gotten fat.

Or was that because he had just come from being with Leona?

"Papa's home," Wanda called out and the children ran to him. He got down on his knees and caught both of them, hugging them tight, but the devil was in him and all he could think about was Leona.

Damn her, and damn him.

Ben Jones had been quiet since they left the trading post. Now they were close to the hideout and he'd still not said a word.

Adam Lee reined in his horse a bit so the others could go ahead, then pulled up alongside Jones.

"You got somethin' ta say?"

Ben Jones's mouth was a slash.

"Come on, spit it out," Lee said.

"You shouldn'ta done it."

"He had it comin'."

"Dat's jus' it, Adam," Jones said. "He didn't have it comin'. He didn't do nothin' ta us."

"He was a white man."

"We can't kill all the white men."

"Why not?" Lee asked. "If we get enough of us together, why not?"

"Because the Indians couldn't do it, and dere's more of them red men den dere are of us."

"But we're smarter den dey are."

"Dat's what Custer thought, too," Jones said.

"You comparin' me to that white cracker Custer?"

Why not? Jones thought. *You both crazy.*

But what he said out loud was, "I'm jus' talkin'."

"You know what?" Lee said. "I liked it better when you wasn't talkin'."

He gigged his horse and rushed up to join the others. Ben Jones went back to riding with his mouth set in a hard slash. He was going to have to tell George what had happened. George would know what to do. He was the smartest one of them all.

Leaving Rector, Clint and Bass Reeves continued to drift to the west, looking for a likely place for a gang to hide out.

"They got families with them," Reeves said. "They're gonna need buildings."

"Something like an abandoned barn," Clint suggested, "or an old line shack."

They continued to ride and then Clint said, "They got children with them?"

"That's what I hear," Reeves said. "Women and children."

"If we come across them away from their camp, they're likely to put up a fight," Clint surmised. "But if we find their camp, maybe they'll give up rather than endanger the women and children."

"I guess that's gonna depend on who's leadin' 'em," Reeves said.

"Bass."

"Yeah?"

"Do you know any of these people?"

It was a question he hadn't asked up to now, but somehow he thought this was the time.

Reeves hesitated, then said, "One of them might be my cousin."

"What's his name?"

"Ben Jones. He's a good boy."

"Why would he be riding with a group that's gone bad?" Clint asked.

"Like I said," Reeves answered. "It'll depend on who's leadin' them. Ben's a good boy, but he ain't no leader. He'd follow somebody who is."

"The judge know you got a cousin riding with this group?" Clint asked.

"I ain't asked," Reeves said, "but there's one thing I know about the judge."

"What's that?"

"He knows everything."

THIRTY

George didn't know where Leona was, or if she had come back from their secret meeting. But he heard the horses approaching, grabbed his rifle, and went outside in case it wasn't the others.

It was, and instantly he knew something had gone wrong. He could tell from Ben Jones's demeanor.

"Ben," Adam Lee yelled, "you take care of all the horses."

Ben was young and was one of the two men who had no wife and no family. George could see in the slump of his shoulders and the set of his jaw that something was eating at him. But he knew he wouldn't have to go and find Ben to learn what was wrong. Eventually, Ben would come to him.

He always did.

"George," Adam Lee said, all smiles, "come over to my shack. I wanna hear what you found out in town."

George and Lee had their own places, but Lee's was an old line shack, and he had a lot more room for him, his wife, and their children.

They stopped outside of the line shack and Lee said, "So?"

George gave his report, which basically was that there were no deputies in town, just the one lawman. The bank looked pretty much the way the two white men said it did, at least from outside.

"What about you?" he asked. "Things go okay?"

"Why wouldn't they?" Lee asked. "We got the supplies we need. Dat should hold us till we gets back from the bank."

"Okay, good," George said.

"Anythin' else?" Lee asked.

"No."

He was trying to look past Lee, to see if Leona was inside. Finally, he heard the kids and saw her moving around.

"George?"

"Huh?"

"I said okay," Lee repeated. "I got to get some rest."

"Oh, okay," George said. "I'll see you later."

Lee gave George a funny look as he turned and left, then went inside to see his kids and give Leona a peck on the cheek. She was wearing one of those dresses again, the ones that made her nipples show. He knew the other men looked at her, and that the women hated her because of it, but he didn't care. He was going to be done with all these people when they got back from that bank job. In fact, tonight he was going to tell Leona his plans.

She was going to be real surprised—and pleased.

As George walked back to his place, Ben Jones came up on him real quick.

"George, we got to talk."

"Okay, Ben," George said. "Come to my place—"

"No," Ben said. "Let's jes' keep walkin'. I don't want nobody else to hear what I got to say."

"Okay."

As they walked, Ben said, "It went wrong at the trading post, George, real wrong."

"I just talked to Adam," George said, "he said everything went okay."

"He killed him, George," Ben said. "He jus' shot him down in cold blood."

"Who, Ben? Who killed who?"

Ben looked around, and even though they had cleared the camp and no one could hear him, he grabbed George's sleeve and pulled him closer.

"Adam killed the man who ran the tradin' post. Jus' shot him for no reason."

"Why would he shoot him for no reason?"

"'Cause he's crazy, that's why," Ben said. "He's talkin' 'bout killin' all white men. Says the black man can do what the red man couldn't."

"What?"

"I'm tellin' ya," Ben said. "He's gone crazy, George."

"Okay, calm down, Ben, calm down."

"I know some people got killed when that stage turnt over, but that wasn't our fault," Ben said. "But this . . . this was cold blood."

"What did the man say to Adam?"

"Just that he always treated our people good."

"And then Adam shot him?"

"Oh, he said somethin' else, I don't remember," Ben said, rubbing his face. "But whatever he said, George, he didn't have to get killed."

"Okay, Ben, okay," George said. "Take it easy."

"You gots to do somethin', George," Ben said.

"I will—"

"You gots to take over."

"Take over?"

"You gots to be the new leader."

"Ben, there's no way Adam would give that up, unless—"

"Unless he was dead," Ben said, "and you gots to do it, George. You gots to kill 'im!"

THIRTY-ONE

Clint and Reeves camped that night near a circle of rocks and large stones that offered plenty of cover. They didn't know how near they were to the black cowboys' hideout, so they didn't want to take a chance of being seen, or even stumbled upon. They made a fire, though, and cooked up some coffee and beans.

"Let 'em come," Reeves groused. "I'm hungry, and I need some coffee."

"I won't argue that," Clint said.

Clint did the cooking because they'd already discovered that his trail coffee was better than the deputy's.

They had a conversation about patience, Clint telling Reeves that he admired his. But when Reeves explained it, it wasn't really something to be admired.

"What else I got to do?" Reeves asked. "If I ride around out here for months trackin' that gang, what do I care?"

Clint realized he was right. This was his job, and if he was riding around in circles out here waiting to bump into them, well, he was being paid for it.

Clint, on the other hand, was not. The amount of time he was willing to put into this was finite. He didn't tell Reeves that, though. No need, he wasn't near that time yet.

But when he got there, he'd let the deputy know.

"What's wrong, George?" Wanda asked.

They were sitting out in front of their lean-to. Inside, the babies slept. Outside, they had built a fire to cook, and now they sat by its warmth.

He looked at his wife. It amazed him how different she looked—again. That afternoon, after being with Leona, she had looked fat and old. Tonight, in the flickering light of the fire, he could see the love she had for him etched on her face, in her eyes, in her smile, in her look of concern. He felt it in her hand as she reached out to touch his arm.

And still he could only think of how Leona's skin felt, how her insides had scalded him when he entered her. She had bewitched him, pure and simple, and there was nothing he could do about it.

"It's Adam," he lied.

"What about him?"

He told her what Ben had told him happened that afternoon at the trading post.

"Maybe Ben's right," she said. "He's a young'n but he's smart."

"Maybe . . ."

"What are you gon' do, George?"

"I don't know."

"What Ben want you to do?"

He looked at her and said, "He wants me to kill Adam Lee and take over."

She rubbed his arm and said, "The others would follow you. You be a better leader than Adam, dat for sho."

"I don't want to be anybody's leader, Wanda."

"You mines," she said. "And you da leader to dose kids in dere."

"Sure," he said. "Look where they're sleepin'."

"Dat ain't yer fault."

"It ain't my fault I can't provide for my family?"

"You doin' what you can," she insisted. "You doin' what you got to do. Cain't nobody fault you for that."

"We broke the law so many times, Wanda," he said. "People died in that stage—"

Calmly, she said, "Dat waren't yer fault neither."

"Maybe not . . . but Adam killed a man in cold blood," he said.

"Are you sho?"

"I talked to a couple of the others," he said. "He did it, all right. White man mouthed off to him. Adam got mad and shot him through the heart."

"Den maybe he is crazy," she said. "Maybe he do need ta be put down."

"I ain't no killer, Wanda," he said. "I ain't no leader neither."

"Well," she said, "even if you don't believe in yo'self, I believes in you." She leaned over and kissed his cheek. He could feel the warmth of her big body through her dress. It used to fill him with a sense of safety. Now it made him long for the heat of Leona's body.

"You stay out here, or go for a walk," she said. "You deal wit' it and den you comes ta bed."

"Okay," he said, " 'night."

"Good night."

She went inside and lay down with the two babies.

He got up, went for a walk, ended up in that clearing among the trees where he and Leona had lain down together.

"I knew you'd come here," Leona said, smiling at him in the dark.

THIRTY-TWO

Clint had taken the second watch, so as first light showed he put on a fresh pot of coffee. By the time he roused Reeves, the coffee was ready.

"Ooh, Lord," Reeves said. "I think your mornin' coffee's even stronger than your nighttime coffee."

"It's got to wake us up," Clint said.

"Well, I do believe after one sip I'm awake," the deputy said.

"Good," Clint said, "because I want to talk to you about something."

"What about?"

"This job we're figuring the black cowboys are going to pull. Do you know of any payrolls that are coming into the area?"

"No," Reeves said, "the only payrolls come from the ranchers, and they get 'em from the banks in Sherman and Paris."

"Anything else going on that you heard about?" Clint asked. "Big high-stakes poker game?"

"No."

"Any kind of shipment of gold or money?"

"No."

"Or something they could sell?"

"I ain't heard of nothin' like that," Reeves said. "'Course, we could go back to Paris or Sherman and ask."

"What about the banks themselves?"

"What about them?"

"Think they'd try to rob the bank in Paris?" Clint asked.

"They'd be crazy," Reeves said.

"Why?"

"Too much law, both local and federal. Hell, the judge's court is there."

"So that leaves Sherman."

"It ain't a big bank."

"Big enough for half a dozen black cowboys to benefit from, right? I mean, what've they got now? The proceeds from each of their jobs is probably gone before they pull the next one."

"So what you're tryin' ta tell me is you think they're gonna hit the bank in Sherman?"

"That's what I'm trying to tell you," Clint said. "What do you think?"

Reeves rubbed his jaw.

"What even makes you think they're plannin' a big job?" he asked.

"How long have they been running around out here pulling small ones?"

"About six months."

"Don't you think it's about time?" Clint asked. "And what about those two guys in the saloon trying to send us on a wild-goose chase?"

"To keep us out of the way?"

"Why else?" Clint asked. "Why even make their presence known to us?"

"Could be another bank."

"You said yourself there isn't one," Clint said, "not big enough. Paris, where there's too much law, and Sherman, where there isn't."

Reeves scratched his head.

"So what's your idea? We just sit on that bank and wait?"

"What's the difference?" Clint said. "Riding around aimlessly out here for days, hoping to bump into them, or waiting in town for a few days, where it's more comfortable?"

"We'd have to make sure nobody knew we were there," Reeves said. "If they heard, they'd never show up."

"I didn't check, but is there a building across the street—a hotel, maybe—that we could watch the bank from?"

"Not right across the street, but there's a hotel where we'd be able to see it from a front window."

"This is your call, Bass," Clint said. "I agreed to help you, and I may be way off on this. You know at least one of the people in that gang. Does your cousin have family?"

"No, he's alone."

"Well, the men with families may be getting impatient," Clint said. "One good job and they could split up and go their separate ways."

"There ain't enough money in that bank to make them rich," Reeves pointed out.

"Forgive me for saying this, but how much money does a black cowboy with no job and a family to feed need to feel rich?"

"You got a point," Reeves said.

"So what do you want to do?"

"I'm still thinkin' we shoulda brought those two men in

and sweated them a little, found out what was on their minds."

"Fine," Clint said. "Let's ride back to Sherman, but go through Rector first. If they're still there, we'll do it. How's that sound?"

"I guess it sounds better than ridin' around out here lookin' for the tracks of an Indian pony to show up again," Reeves admitted.

"I'll get the fire," Clint said, "you get the horses."

THIRTY-THREE

George Washington woke up the next morning, hoping that the smell of Leona wasn't still on him. He had come back last night, found his family asleep, and then lay down as far away from them as possible, which wasn't very far in the lean-to. It was barely larger than a jail cell, and he'd been in jail, so he knew.

He woke first and sneaked out to go wash in a nearby stream. The reason this site had been a good choice for them were the various buildings—even though they were falling down—and the stream.

He took off his shirt and washed his chest, arms and armpits, face and neck as thoroughly as he could. Then he looked around and dropped his trousers to wash his genitals. He and his wife had not been intimate since they took possession of the lean-to—it was not something you could do with the kids in there—but he wanted to be careful. If his wife smelled another woman on him, she'd know who it was. He was sure of that. Bad enough she already referred to Leona as "that ho'."

He couldn't wash his trousers because he had to wear them, but he rinsed his shirt thoroughly, smelled it, then did it again. It was hard to get the sex stink of Leona off it without soap.

"'Mornin'."

He jumped and turned around, eyes wide. Adam Lee was standing there, watching him wash the smell of his wife off. He was unarmed, and so was George.

"Guess you had the same idea as me, huh?" Lee asked. "I been smellin' kinda ripe."

Without waiting for an answer, Lee knelt by the water and did the same thing George had done just moments before, taking off his shirt and washing himself thoroughly. Lee's body was a collection of bones with very little skin. Even though George was unarmed, he could have killed the man easily right then and there. As Lee bent over the water, George could have just pushed his face in and held it there, or he could have broken his neck. But would he be doing it because of what Ben Jones told him? Because the man had gone crazy? Or would he just be getting Lee out of the way so he could have his wife? And if he needed to kill Adam Lee to be with Leona, what about Wanda?

Lee took his face out of the water and shook his head like a dog.

"God, dat be cold!"

He dried his face with his shirt, not bothering to wash it.

"George," he said, turning to face the man he thought was his friend, his second-in-command, "we gotta talk about when to take dat bank."

"The sooner the better, I say," George said. "This bunch is going stir-crazy, bein' around each other for so long, livin' like this."

"Yeah," Lee said, "you may be right, but we got a good thing goin' here, ya know?"

"Whadaya mean? This . . . this is God awful."

"No, no . . . I mean, yeah, the livin' conditions is awful, but after we rob dat bank, we'll have the money to set our families up comfortable-like, and then we can get back to work."

"Back to work?"

"Banks," Lee said. "Once we rob this one, we'll be able to keep doin' it."

"Adam," George said, standing up, "this was supposed to be somethin' we did ta get back on our feet. Somethin' temporary. I ain't no bank robber, and neither is Ben or the others."

Adam Lee chuckled.

"Don't fool yerself, George," he said. "We all bank robbers now."

"And killers, too?" George demanded.

"What?"

"I heard what you did yesterday."

Lee shook out his shirt and averted his eyes.

"I don't know what you talkin' about."

"Yeah, ya do," George said. "You shot down that white man in cold blood."

"You didn't hear what he said to me."

"We're killin' white men now for what they say?" George asked. "We better have a lot of goddamned bullets, then."

"Yeah, we should," Lee said, facing George now. "We should kill as many white men as we can."

"Rob banks, kill white men," George said, "kill white women!"

"Dat woman in the stage, dat was an accident," Lee pointed out defensively, "but white is white."

"White women, Adam? What have we become?"

"We what dey made us," Lee said. "I thought you understand that, George, but maybe you ain't as smart as you supposed ta be."

George didn't say anything.

"Oh, yeah, I know what some of de others say," Lee went on, "dat you should be the leader 'cause you de smart one. You wan' be de leader, George?"

Again, George didn't speak.

"'Cause if dat's what you want, you gon' have ta kill me." Lee pounded his scrawny chest. "Come on, you bigger den me, you stronger den me, you smarter den me . . . come kill me and be de leader."

"I don't want to kill you, Adam."

"No," Lee said, "'cause you ain't a leader, George. You a follower."

He started to walk away from the stream, toward the camp, then turned back.

"You a follower, like de rest of dem sheep," he said, pointing back toward camp. "And you'll all do what I say—and I say we robbin' dat bank, and den another one, and den another . . ."

George watched him walk away and thought maybe Ben was right. Maybe Lee had gone crazy, and maybe somebody should take care of him and replace him as leader.

Maybe he'd missed the chance to kill Lee. But if another chance came, he was going to be ready.

THIRTY-FOUR

Clint and Bass Reeves rode back into Rector that afternoon. They dismounted in front of the same saloon and went inside. It was slow and the bartender was alone except for one drunk with his head down on a table, an empty bottle of whiskey next to him.

"Remember us?" Clint asked.

The bartender looked at them and said, "Sure, the marshals. What'll ya have?"

"Information," Reeves said.

"'Bout what?" the man asked.

"Two men," Reeves said. "They were sittin' over there." He pointed.

"I seen lots of men—"

"These two came over and talked to us while they got fresh beers," Reeves said.

The bartender scratched his balding head, then his protruding stomach.

"Sorry—"

"You remember," Reeves said coldly.

"Look, Marshal—"

"Deputy," Reeves said, tapping the badge.

"Okay, Deputy, I don't wanna get in no trouble with those fellas—"

"To stay out of trouble with them fellas," Reeves said, "you have ta get in trouble with me and my friend here."

"You don't want to do that," Clint asked, "now do you?"

The bartender looked from one to the other, then sighed.

"No. What do you want to know?"

"Who were they?"

"Don't know."

"Where'd they go?"

"I don't know."

"Are they still in town?"

"I don't know."

They glared at him.

"Hey, ask me a question I know the answer to and I'll answer it."

"Did they leave right after we did yesterday?" Clint asked.

"That I can answer," the man said happily. "No, they stayed and had a few more beers and then left."

"Did you see which way they went when they went out those doors?" Reeves asked.

The man thought a moment, then said, "I think they turned left."

"Now maybe we're getting somewhere," Clint said. "Is there a hotel that way?"

"Yeah," the bartender said.

"Which one?"

"The only one in town."

"Okay," Clint said. "Thanks."

They left the saloon, turned left, and walked into the lobby of the hotel. The desk clerk did a double take when he saw the big black man, then spotted the badge.

"Can I help ya, Marshal?"

"Deputy," Reeves said, tapping the badge. *He's being particular today*, Clint thought.

"Yes, sir," the young clerk said. "What can I do for you today, Deputy?"

"Two white men," Reeves said. "Did they check out?"

"Which two white men?"

"How many white men checked out last night or to-day?" Clint asked.

"Two."

"At the same time?"

"Yes, they were together."

"In one room?"

"Yes."

"And did they sign the register?"

"Sure."

Clint grabbed the book and turned it around. There were only two check-ins that week: Arch Wilson and Denny Radke.

"Gotta be them," Reeves said.

"Did you hear them say anythin' about where they were goin'?" Reeves asked.

"They didn't say a word in front of me," the clerk said.

"Damn it," Clint said.

"But I noticed they stopped just outside the door and had a conversation, then moved on."

"So?" Clint asked.

"Andy was out there, sittin' in a chair."

"And?" Reeves asked.

"He might've heard what they said."

"Might've?" Reeves asked.

"Well," the clerk said, "Andy's the town drunk. He would've had to be awake . . ."

"And where do we find this Andy?" Reeves asked.

"Let me guess," Clint said. "The saloon."

"Yep."

"What's he look like?" Reeves asked.

"You'll recognize him," the clerk said. "By this time of the day he usually has his head down on the table."

THIRTY-FIVE

They retraced their steps to the saloon and, as soon as they entered, the bartender said, "I tol' ya all I know, I swear."

"We're not here for you," Reeves said.

All three men looked at the man whose head was slumped on his table.

"Andy?" the bartender said.

"Andy," Reeves said.

"What's your name?" Clint asked.

"Jake."

"How bad is he?" Clint said.

"Pretty bad," the bartender said, "but it's a funny thing about Andy, even when he's this bad, you can get him to make sense."

"How?" Clint asked.

"Two ways," Jake said. "Money, or another bottle."

Reeves looked at Clint, who said, "Both?" He put his hand in his pocket and came out with a dollar.

"I'll get a bottle," Reeves said.

Clint walked over to the table and dropped the dollar coin on it. It didn't sound that loud to him, but to the man with his head on the table it must have been plenty loud. His head jerked up immediately, but eyes were only half open.

Reeves came over with the new bottle of whiskey and slapped it down on the table. That, and the smell, brought Andy's eyes open the rest of the way.

"Well, gentlemen," he said, looking up at them, "won't you join me for a little libation?"

Clint was surprised. Andy sounded like a well-educated drunk. He was in his fifties, with nothing but wisps of hair left on his head, and a permanent five-o'clock shadow on his face. It wasn't warm in the saloon, but he was already sweating alcohol from his pores.

"Andy," Clint said, "we're not going to share this bottle of whiskey with you."

"You're not?" He looked like he was going to cry.

"No," Reeves said, "we're gonna give you the whole bottle, and this dollar, all for yourself."

"Well, gentlemen, that's very kind of you, to treat a stranger with such—"

"But not yet," Reeves said, pulling the bottle away as Andy reached for it while Clint did the same with the dollar.

"I-I don't understand." Andy looked confused.

"We'll clear it up for you," Clint said. "Earlier today you were in front of the hotel. Two men came out and had a conversation. We want to know what they said."

Andy closed his eyes for a moment, then opened them and spoke.

"One said to the other, 'I thought we was gonna stay in

town longer,' and the other one said, 'Well, I do the thinkin' and I got an idea last night,' and the first one said, 'So where are we goin'?' and the other one said, 'We're headin' back to Sherman,' and the first one said, 'What for?' and the second one said, 'I'll let you know when we get there.' " Andy closed his eyes again, then opened them, and smiled at them. "Now can I have it?"

Clint and Reeves were staring at him in wonderment.

"Are you sure that's what they said?" Clint asked.

"Word for word, sir," Andy answered. "My memory is perfect."

"Even drunk?" Reeves asked.

"Even better," Andy said. "I simply have to close my eyes and dispel the fog and the words come to me. It's a gift, gentlemen, a gift. And speaking of gifts . . ."

Reeves handed him the bottle and Clint handed him the dollar, then took another from his pocket and added that to the booty.

"You earned it."

"Gentlemen, I thank you from the bottom of my heart."

As they left the saloon, Andy took a long swallow from the bottle, then placed it on the table and put his head down, right on top of the two one-dollar coins. Clint figured by the time he lifted it again he'd have the impression of the two coins on his forehead.

"Toldja," the bartender said as they left.

Outside, Reeves said to Clint, "That was amazing."

"Well, we know they're heading back to Sherman," Clint said.

"But we don't know for what."

"Something's going to happen there."

"Then I guess we'd better make sure we're there when it does."

They stepped down from the walk, mounted their horses, and once again rode out of Rector, but this time in a different direction.

THIRTY-SIX

Arch Wilson and Denny Radke rode into the black cowboy camp, sat their horses, and waited. Suddenly, they were surrounded by six black men with rifles.

"What de hell you doin' here?" Adam Lee demanded. "How you find us?"

"I guess you fellas can't tell when you're bein' followed."

"Yeah, we followed you last time," Radke said. "You didn't even know it."

"Ya'll goin' get yo'selves killed," Ben Jones warned.

"Take it easy," George Washington said, "everybody just take it easy." He pointed his handgun to the ground.

Wilson pointed at George and said, "Now, he's the smartest of you all. Listen to him."

George was sure Lee didn't like hearing that.

"I'm just sayin' let's don't all get killed," George said. "Let's hear what they got to say."

"Yeah," Wilson said, stepping down from his horse, "let's palaver."

Behind him, Radke dismounted.

"You're the leader, right?" he asked, pointing at Adam Lee.

"Dat's right."

"So let's talk," he said. "How about you, him, and us." He pointed at George.

"Ya'll go on back to your families," Lee said to the rest of them. "Come on, George."

"I ain't got no family," Ben Jones said.

"And you wanna live long enough to get one, right?" Wilson asked, making a shooing motion at Jones.

"Go ahead, Ben," George said.

Reluctantly, Ben Jones moved off.

Lee and George moved in closer to the two white men.

"We're here to help you, so don't go gettin' all riled up on us," Wilson said.

"Whatchoo got to say?" Lee asked.

"We were in Rector yesterday," Wilson said. "You know Rector?"

"Yeah, it's a small town near Sherman."

"Right," Wilson said. "Well, yesterday we saw a deputy marshal there."

"Black one?" George asked.

"That's right."

"Bass Reeves," Lee said. "What did he want?"

"Well, we guessed he was lookin' for you, so we sent him lookin' south. We don't want him gettin' in the way when you decide to take your bank, do we?"

"South? You sent them south?"

"That's right. So you better get on your horses and get to that bank soon, 'cause they ain't gonna be ridin' south forever."

"And that's what we came here ta tell you," Radke said.

"So we followed you, so what? We ain't gonna tell anybody where you are."

"No," Lee said, "you ain't."

He raised his rifle and, as soon as the two white men realized what he was going to do, they went for their guns. This eventuality had just never occurred to them.

"Hey, wha—" Arch Wilson managed to say before Lee shot him in the chest.

"Son of a—" Denny Radke said, but George, acting on instinct, shot him dead before he could get anything else out, or get his gun clear of leather.

The two white men lay on their backs in the dirt, dead.

"Damn it, Adam," George said.

"Hey, you did good, George."

"I didn't have much choice, did I?" George asked. "What'd you go and do that for?"

"You heard dem, and you saw dem," Lee said. "They followed us here, they could tell the law where we was."

"You think they would've? They wouldn't've done a thing until after the bank job."

"And we woulda had to kill them anyway, 'cause they was plannin' ta take the money from us. You know dat, George."

Grudgingly, George said, "I know it."

"So dey dead sooner den later," Lee said.

The others came running and stopped short when they saw the two dead men.

"Get these two men buried," Lee said, "far away from here, though."

"How far?" Ben Jones asked.

"Hell, t'row dem on their horses and take 'em out far. Den bury 'em."

"Okay," Jones said, "okay." He waved at the other men and the four of them loaded the dead men onto their horses and then started walking. One of them veered off, grabbed two shovels, and ran to catch up.

"What about Bass Reeves?" Lee asked George. "You think dese two was tellin' the truf?"

"Yeah, I do," George said. "I think right now Mr. Reeves is ridin' south."

"Then we goin' in ta take dat bank tomorrow, George," Lee said. "You wit' us, right?"

"Yeah, Adam," George said, "I'm with you."

THIRTY-SEVEN

Clint and Reeves stopped just outside of Sherman.

"There's no way we can ride into town unnoticed," Clint said. "You're just too big to miss."

"And too black."

"You said it, not me."

"I know it. So you go in and you get a room at that hotel, a front room."

"If they've got one."

"They'll have one," Reeves said. "That hotel ain't gonna be full. And if they ain't got one, you make 'em move somebody."

"With my gun?"

Reeves hesitated, then unpinned his badge and passed it to Clint.

"With this."

"I don't want this, Bass."

"Then give it back to me next time you see me," the badgeless deputy said.

"When will you come into town?"

"I'll see if I can sneak around behind some buildings," Reeves said. "Otherwise I'll come in after dark. How am I gonna find your room?"

"I'll hang something on the doorknob."

"Like what?"

"You got a bandana in your saddlebags?"

"Yeah, I do," Reeves pulled out a black one and handed it over.

"I'll wrap this around the doorknob."

"Do me a favor," Reeves said.

"Yeah?"

"Get a room with two beds."

Clint nodded and headed into town.

"You ain't never killed a man before," Wanda said to George.

"I know."

"Not like that."

"I know!" George said.

"If you hadn't you'd be dead," she said, "Adam, too. You didn't have no choice, George."

George thought about it. If he'd been a beat slower, maybe Adam Lee would be dead. Then he'd have had a clear path with Leona. But even though he'd never killed a man before, he'd acted out of instinct, without even thinking about it.

He stepped outside the lean-to.

"Where you goin'?" she asked.

"Just for a walk."

"You takin' lots of walks lately," she said. "You mind if I comes wit' you?"

He did mind but he said, "No."

At that moment the two children got into a dispute over something.

"Never mind," she said. "I gots to take care of dese children."

"I'm gonna make sure Ben and the others got the dead men good and buried."

"You be sure dey buried dem deep, George," she said.

"All right, Wanda."

He walked away from her and from the lean-to, away from his family, and just wanted to keep going. He was getting tired of the responsibility he had, and of the extra responsibilities others were trying to add to his burden.

He was getting tired of all of it—all but Leona.

THIRTY-EIGHT

The doorknob turned after dark and Bass Reeves quickly entered the room, removing the bandana from the door. He turned and looked at the two beds, one of which Clint was reclining on.

"You got a front room with two beds," he said with satisfaction.

"I did have to flash your badge to get the front room," Clint said. "The clerk had to move a man and his wife, ended up giving them a bigger room so they wouldn't complain."

"And the beds?"

"Told him I needed two in case I brought more than one girl up here."

"And is he gonna keep his mouth shut?"

"I hope so," Clint said. "I threatened him enough. Here, take this back. It's too heavy for me."

"I doubt that," Reeves said, taking back his badge and pinning it onto his shirt.

He walked to the window and looked out at the street. The saloon was lit up, and there was enough moonlight to see the front of the bank just down the street.

"We can see it from here, and get to it quick enough," he said.

"You got a deck of cards?" Clint asked.

"No, why?"

"I thought we might play cards for a while, since we're going to be cooped up in here."

"No reason for both of us to be cooped up," Reeves said. "I'm the one who's gonna attract the attention. As long as nobody knows who you are—or remembers that we were together—you can go out, get us some food, and come back with a deck of cards."

Clint swung his feet off the bed and said, "That's a damned good idea." He stood up, still fully dressed and wearing his gun. "Hopefully, I can find some place that serves food this late."

"Should be one or two places," Reeves said. "Just be careful ya don't run into that Sheriff Burton. You'll have ta explain what you're doin' here."

"I'll tell him we had a falling-out," Clint said. "You went your way, I went mine."

"He'll believe that," Reeves said, "especially if you tell him, 'You know how those people are.' "

Burton hadn't struck Clint as a racist, just something of a fool, but he didn't argue.

"I'll be back with as much as I can get," Clint said. "Too bad this hotel doesn't have a dining room."

"I'll bet the clerk can tell ya where ta get some food," Reeves said, lying with his back on the bed. "This hotel's got good mattresses, for a fleabag."

"Just don't get used to it," Clint said.

"Hmmm?" Reeves asked, eyes closed.

"I'll be back," Clint said, and stepped out into the hall.

Clint found a café that was about a half a minute from clos-ing. The waiter made him a batch of sandwiches and wrapped them up in a red napkin for him to carry.

"You wouldn't happen to have a deck of cards, would you?" Clint asked.

"Sorry, no," the man said. "Try the saloon."

"Yeah, thanks."

Clint knew he could get a deck from the saloon, but he was trying to avoid going in there. He stopped outside the café for a minute, while the waiter locked the door behind him. He looked up and down the street, then figured, how much trouble could he get into just asking for a deck of cards?

He headed for the saloon.

The saloon was crowded, but when Clint Adams entered through the batwing doors he was recognized.

"Damn, damn," Pete Rickard said, nudging his friend, Ollie Evans. "You see what I see?"

"What?"

"Not what. Who? It's Clint Adams."

"The Gunsmith?"

"In the flesh," Rickard said.

"You been lookin' for him," Ollie said.

"For years," Rickard said.

"You gonna kill 'im?"

"Damn right I am," Rickard said. "That there is my rep-utation, Ollie. I ain't gettin' any younger."

"You're twenty-two, like me," Ollie said with a frown.

"Never mind," Rickard said, "just back my play."

"You're the fastest man I ever seen with a gun, Pete," Ollie said. "Why you need me backin' ya?' "

"Because it's a crowded saloon and I don't aim to get back-shot. Understand?"

"I understand. Watch your back."

"Right," Rickard said. "Let's go."

THIRTY-NINE

Clint elbowed his way to the bar, careful to keep the sandwiches from being crushed, and got the bartender's attention.

"Can I get a deck of cards?"

"What for?"

"Play some solitaire in my hotel room."

"I can't give ya a new deck."

"That's okay, a used deck would be good."

"Lemme look around. You want a beer while you're waitin'?"

"No, thanks."

"Suit yerself," the bartender said with a shrug.

Clint nodded and the man went off to find a deck.

"Hey!"

Somebody poked him in the back.

Great.

He turned and looked over his shoulder at a young man in his early twenties. He had the look. Clint was fifty-fifty in these situations. Sometimes he was able to talk them out of it. Sometimes he wasn't. Tonight he didn't feel like trying.

"I know you," the man said.

"I don't know you," Clint said, and turned his head back to the bar.

"I said I know you, Clint Adams!" the boy shouted.

Suddenly, it got quiet. The one time Clint could have used a noisy piano.

The men on either side of Clint melted away, giving him some room to turn.

"Son," he said, "I just came in here for a deck of cards, not trouble."

"What's that?" the kid asked, indicating the sandwiches. "You goin' on a picnic?"

"Taking some food back to my room, with a deck of cards, to play some solitaire," Clint said. "All these people can hear me trying to get out of this, kid."

"Tryin' to back out, you mean. 'Cause you're yella," the kid said.

"Names don't bother me, kid."

"Don't call me kid," the kid said. "My name's Pete Rickard and I've killed ten men."

"Good for you."

"I been lookin' for you for years, Adams."

Clint laughed. He couldn't help it.

"Kid, you ain't been alive for years."

Laughter erupted around them and the kid flushed a deep red. Clint knew he'd blown any chance he might have had to get out of this without trouble.

"Okay, kid, look—"

"No, you look," Rickard said. "I'm gonna count to three and draw, and you better be ready."

"What if I draw on two?"

That stumped the kid.

"What?"

"I said what if I draw on two and you draw on three. You'll be dead."

"T-that ain't fair."

"Life ain't fair, kid." Clint looked around, saw that they were the center of attention. He pointed to one of the saloon girls—a cute blonde—and called her over.

"Yeah?" she said nervously.

"Hold these for me, will you, sweetie?" Clint asked, handing her the sandwiches. "I don't want anything to happen to them."

"O-okay."

She melted back into the crowd, cradling the sandwiches to her breasts.

"Okay, kid," Clint said. "I'm ready. Go ahead and count."

"B-but are you gonna wait for three?"

"Who knows?" Clint asked. "I may draw on one."

"B-but—"

Clint drew his gun and stuck it in the boy's face. Nobody in the room had seen his hand move. He never did this, never drew his gun unless he was going to use it, but he didn't want to kill this kid, not tonight. If he did, he'd have to deal with the law, and Bass Reeves was waiting back in the room.

"Maybe I won't wait for you to count at all."

The kid's eyes crossed as he looked down the barrel. He licked his lips nervously.

"Now can I go and eat my sandwiches?" he asked.

The kid nodded.

"Where are my sandwiches?" Clint called out.

"Here."

The girl came running over and put them in Clint's free hand.

"And where's my deck?"

"Here," the bartender said. He came over and stuck the deck in the same hand. "I, uh, gave you a new deck, Mr. Adams."

"Thanks."

"Anything else?" the man asked.

"Well, since you're asking, how about a bottle of whiskey?"

"Comin' up."

The bartender rushed to the bar, got a bottle, and brought it back.

"On the house."

"Thanks. Hey, kid, your buddy over there isn't going to try to back-shoot me when I walk out, is he?"

"N-no."

"That's good." He turned to the door. "I need a path, please."

Everybody shifted and made a path for him to the batwings.

"Thanks."

Clint walked to the door, keeping a wary eye on Rickard and his friend, gun still in hand. It wasn't until he was outside that he holstered it.

He opened the door to the room, entered, and tossed the wrapped sandwiches to Reeves, who caught them.

"Anything to drink?"

Clint showed him the bottle of whiskey.

"I just need enough to wash the food down," Reeves said.

"Me, too."

"No glasses?"

"We'll just pass the bottle back and forth."

Reeves stared at him.

"You don't mind drinkin' from the same bottle as me?" he asked.

"Does your black rub off?" Clint asked. "No, I don't mind. Maybe you mind drinking from the same bottle as me?"

"Naw," Reeves said, "I'll just wipe it with my sleeve. Did you get some cards?"

Clint sat on his bed and held them up.

"I got 'em. Poker?"

"Sure," Reeves said, untying the sandwiches, "after we eat."

They each took a sandwich and Reeves said, "Did you have any trouble?"

"Trouble?" Clint asked. "No, no trouble."

FORTY

The morning sun woke both of them, streaming in the window and across their beds.

"Bank don't open till nine," Reeves said.

"They don't have to wait for the bank to open to rob it," Clint said.

"That's true," Reeves said. "I knew I'd like this damned bed too much. Don't wanna get up."

"Neither do I," Clint said. "We got any sandwiches left?"

Reeves turned his head and opened his eyes. There were two sandwiches on the table between them.

"Two, and some whiskey."

"Whiskey and sandwiches for breakfast?" Clint grimaced. "Great."

"You could go out for some breakfast."

"I got lucky last night," Clint said. "Don't want to push my luck."

"Whadaya mean?"

Clint told him about the kid in the saloon.

"You said you didn't have no trouble."

"I didn't, not really," Clint said. "Just a snot-nosed kid. I was more worried about something happening to the sandwiches."

Reeves sat up in bed.

"So the word is out that you're in town."

"I guess it is."

"You're gonna have to go and talk to the sheriff."

"Why?"

"Because he might start lookin' for you," Reeves said. "We don't need him gettin' in the way at the wrong time."

"So I go and find him, and tell him our falling-out story."

"And then he stops lookin', maybe even leaves you alone."

"Okay," Clint said, "then that means I've got to get up."

"And I don't," Reeves said, lying back down. "Listen, while you're out, why don't you get some breakfast and bring it back?"

"Yeah, yeah," Clint said. "That's me, errand boy."

"Better you than me, white man," Reeves said. Clint could hear the smile in his voice.

Clint left the hotel and went directly to the sheriff's office. As he waked in, Burton looked up at him and grinned laconically.

"You saved me the trouble of havin' to come and find you," he said.

"I figured you would've heard what happened last night by now."

"Sounds like you humiliated the little shit," Burton said, shaking his head. "Wish I coulda been there to see it."

"There wasn't much to it."

Burton chuckled and said, "That's not the way I heard it. So what happened to your buddy, Reeves?"

Clint shrugged.

"He went his way, I went mine."

"I got respect for the judge, and for the badge, but why he ever put it on a nigger is beyond me."

Clint didn't comment.

"So what brings you back to Sherman?"

Clint shrugged.

"Just heading back the way I came."

"Staying long?"

"I'm letting my horse get some rest," Clint said. "I'll probably move on in a couple of days."

"That big stallion of yours needs rest?"

"Well, if he doesn't, I do."

"Reeves still out there tryin' ta track that gang?" Burton asked.

"I suppose."

"Seems to me a buncha black cowboys playin' outlaw shouldn't be so hard to find."

"You think they're playing?"

"You heard what happened with that stagecoach?" Burton asked. "That never woulda happened with an experienced gang. Yeah, I think they're playin' bad guy, and it won't go on much longer."

"Why's that?"

"Because sooner or later they're gonna bite off more than they can chew," Burton said. "Like if they came here."

"Here?"

"Yeah. Let's say they wanted to rob the bank here. I'd scatter them like sheep."

"Just you? No deputies?"

"I don't need any deputies for a bunch of niggers, Adams," Burton said. "You wait and see. They'll either shoot themselves in the foot or just scatter and get lost for good. They ain't gonna last much longer."

"Well," Clint said, "it's no skin off my nose either way. I'm going to hole up in my room for a couple of days and get some rest. I'm not looking for any excitement."

Burton chuckled again.

"You mean like last night?"

"I mean exactly like last night," Clint said. "The last thing I need is to kill another snot-nosed kid who thinks he's Billy the Kid."

"I hear ya," Burton said. "Men like you and me, we got better things to do."

Clint bit his lip—both lips—and left.

FORTY-ONE

Clint returned to the room with sandwiches again, these made from bacon and eggs. He also managed to convince the waiter at the café—who was the same as last night—to let him have a pot of coffee and two mugs. He promised to bring them back later in the day.

While they sat on their beds and ate, Clint said, "You know, this would be a good idea for hotels."

"What would?"

"Sending food up to the rooms," Clint said. "People could order what they want, and eat it in their rooms. They could call it . . . room service, or something like that."

"I don't think the maids would like that idea," Reeves said. "It would be pretty messy."

"Well," Clint said, "I still think it's a good idea."

"Open a hotel and do it," Reeves said.

"Oh, yeah, that's what I want to be," Clint said, "a hotel owner. I'd be more likely to own a saloon."

"I don't see you doin' none of that," Reeves said. "You the kind of man who's gonna die in the saddle."

"Well, there's something to look forward to."

Clint was sitting on his bed eating while Reeves had put a chair by the window and was eating there, keeping his eyes on the bank at the same time.

"What about you, Bass?"

"Whadaya mean?"

"What are you going to do after you take off your badge?"

"Who says I'm gonna take it off?" the black man asked. "I figure ta die with it on. Maybe not this badge, but a badge." He turned and looked at Clint. "I ain't got nothin' else."

"You've got a wife and a family."

"I ain't the kinda man who can jus' sit home with my wife and children," Bass Reeves said. "I guess that makes me a bad husband and father, but it also makes me a damned good lawman."

"I can't argue that point," Clint said.

"Bank's opening," Reeves said.

Clint got up, walked to the window, and looked out over Reeves's head.

"We'd have to be extremely lucky for them to come and hit the bank today," Clint said.

"Damn lucky," Reeves agreed.

Adam Lee instructed all of the women to lock everything up while the men were gone.

"When we get back we'll be movin' out fast," he told them.

"How we gon' move fast with the kids?" Wanda Washington asked. "We ain't got but one buckboard for all of 'em."

"Dat be up to each individual person," Lee said. "You

puts 'em on a horse if you gots to, but we be movin', dat's fo' damn sure."

George wasn't so sure Lee's idea was a good one. Chances were good they'd be leaving Sherman dogged by a posse. Did they want to lead a posse back here to their families?

He wanted to pull Lee aside and suggest a change in plans but the man was in full leader mode, shouting orders and not listening to anyone. So he decided to talk later to the women himself.

While Lee was seeing to the saddling of the horses, George went over to talk to Wanda and Leona because the other wives would listen to them.

"You get these kids ready to travel, put them on the buckboard, and light out. Don't wait for us to get back."

"What about Adam—" Leona started.

"I'll take care of him, don't worry," George said. He wished Leona would stop throwing hot looks his way in front of his wife. "The other women will listen to you two. Get 'em all out of here, because when we leave town we might have a posse on our heels."

"But where do we go?" Wanda asked.

"You remember the last place we camped before we come here?" he asked.

"No—" Leona started, but Wanda cut her off.

"I remember. There was an abandoned barn there. We almost decided to camp there."

"That's right. Go there and wait. I'll come for you when I can. Take all the supplies we have with you. You both got rifles?"

They nodded.

He felt awkward hugging Wanda in front of Leona, especially since he kept getting those looks from Lee's wife.

"Don't worry," Leona said as he started to walk away, "I'll take care of everything here."

The next thing George did was to pull Ben Jones aside and talk to him.

"Listen," he said to the younger man, "we're gonna do this bank thing, but after that we're gonna have to get rid of Adam."

"Get rid of him?"

"Kill him, Ben," George said. "We're gonna have to kill him."

"I can't do that, George," Jones said. "I can't just . . . kill a man. Not in cold blood like that, anyway."

"Don't worry," George said, "I'll take care of it."

"You gon' take over, George?" Ben Jones asked. "Dat what you gon' do?"

"That's what I'm gonna do, but I have a suggestion for you, Ben."

"What?"

"You go find your cousin, Bass Reeves, and throw yourself on his mercy," George said. "You ain't got a family out here like the rest of us. You only got to take care of yourself."

"Well . . ."

"Well, what, Ben?"

Jones looked around to make sure nobody could hear.

"I got to tell you somethin'."

"What?"

"Well . . . it's about one of the women—not Wanda," he hurriedly added.

"What are you tryin' ta say, Ben?"

"I been with . . . Leona."

George felt as if he'd been struck by lightning.

"I mean, I know she older den me, but we in love," the younger man said. "Her husband, he don't treat her good and—oh, lord, George, you don't know what it like bein' wit' a woman like dat. I mean . . . I ain't been wit' a lot of women—"

"Stop," George said.

"What?"

"Just stop talkin'," George said. "You crazy, Ben. She don't love you, she jus' usin' you."

"She ain't not!"

"Ben," George said, "forget about Leona. Adam will kill you if he finds out."

"Yeah," Ben Jones said, "but you gonna kill Adam, so where's the harm? Ya see? You helpin' all of us more den you know."

He slapped George on the back and went to saddle his horse. George felt as if his feet were stuck in the ground. If Leona had been with him, and with Ben . . . how many of the other men had she been with?

FORTY-TWO

Adam Lee reined in his horse and everyone behind him stopped as they came within sight of Sherman, Texas.

"We can't ride in together," he said. "I'll go first, Rafe and Lou next, and George, you and Otis come in last."

"What about me?" Ben Jones asked.

"You ride in right after me, Ben," Lee said. "If Bass Reeves is in town, he'll see you and try to talk to you. Dat's when you gets the jump on him and we takes him."

"Are you still thinkin' about that crazy plan to take Bass Reeves?" George asked.

"It ain't crazy," Lee said. "We got his cousin right here and dat gon' get the jump on him."

"Adam—" Jones started, but Lee cut him off.

"You got to do yer part, boy!" he snapped.

"Yes, sir."

"Good," Lee said. "I'm goin' in first. Any man who don't come in after me, I gon' hunt down and kill. Ya'll understan'?"

They all nodded.

"Let's go," he said to his horse.

"Black man ridin' in," Reeves said.

"We can't suspect every black man we see, Bass," Clint said from the bed.

Reeves turned and looked at Clint.

"You sure you're a white man?"

"That's what they tell me."

Reeves turned back to the window.

"What's he doing?" Clint asked.

"Just ridin' in."

"Armed?"

"Looks like he got a rifle."

"Did he look at the bank?"

"I don't know," Reeves said, "but he's lookin' around."

"Well, if he's one of them, then they're coming in separately, which is smart. They'd attract too much attention if they came in altogether."

"Well, I guess we'll just hafta keep watchin' then," Reeves said.

"And I might as well start my shift now."

George watched Ben Jones ride off in the wake of Adam Lee. He didn't have time to talk to the younger man, so he had no idea what would happen if Bass Reeves was in town. They were just going to have to wait and see.

Ben Jones's heart was beating fast and hard—so much so that he thought it might leap out of his chest. If his cousin Bass was in Sherman, he didn't know what he was going to do. He needed George to kill Adam Lee before that would happen, but it was too late for that.

• • •

"Another black man," Clint said. "Looks like this might be it."

"If they gonna come in one at a time, it's gonna take a while."

"Maybe they're not in a rush," Clint said. "This one's kind of young, tall and lanky, wearing a handgun and riding a gray—"

Bass Reeves exploded off the bed and banged into Clint's back as he rushed to the window.

"Aw, Jesus—" he said.

"What?"

"That's Ben," he said. "That's my cousin."

Clint turned and looked over his shoulder at Bass Reeves.

"How do you want to play this?"

"Stupid little fool," Reeves said. "He's gonna get himself killed for sure."

"You want to go down and get him?"

Reeves backed away from the window. Clint turned back and watched the young man continue to ride in. He didn't know where the first black man had gone, maybe to the livery stable.

"I should let him live with his mistake," Reeves said. "Maybe he'll learn a lesson."

"Yeah, but he'll have to survive in order to live with his mistake," Clint pointed out.

"Ah," Reeves said in disgust, "I don't go down and get him and he gets killed, I'll never hear the end of it from my wife."

"Go ahead," Clint said. "I'll stay here and keep watch."

"Clint—"

"You do what you gotta do, Bass," Clint said.

The other man nodded and left the room.

FORTY-THREE

Ben Jones did as he had been instructed to do. He rode past the bank, kept going, and stopped in front of the first saloon he came to. He glanced around, did not see Adam Lee, and did not see Bass Reeves.

He thought about going into the saloon to get a drink, but he knew from past history that was asking for trouble. None of the white men inside would appreciate his presence. He wondered if Adam Lee was in the saloon. The white men wouldn't scare him none.

He looked around again. Why would Bass Reeves be here? Didn't the two dead white men say they had sent Reeves south? If he was here, it would just be a huge coincidence.

Jones looked up the street, hoping to see George riding in, but there was no sign of him. All he had to do was hang onto his nerves until George showed up.

Suddenly, he saw a figure striding toward him, coming across the street, a big black man with wide shoulders and big hands.

Bass Reeves.

• • •

Adam Lee watched from the alley next to the saloon as Deputy Marshal Bass Reeves closed the ground between himself and his cousin, Ben Jones.

This is gonna work, he thought.

He drew his gun and waited . . .

"Ben!"

"H-hey, Bass—"

"Son, what the hell you doin'?" Reeves demanded of his young cousin.

"Whadaya talk—"

"Don't play stupid with me, boy!" Reeves said. "You ridin' with that gang of black cowboys, that's what I mean."

"Bass, look, you gotta—"

"And now you're here in town to what? Rob the bank?"

Ben Jones's eyes got real big and Reeves knew that Clint was right. They were going to hit the bank.

"Boy, lemme tell you—"

Ben Jones's hand shook as he touched his gun, but he could not bring himself to pull it on his own flesh and blood.

"Bass, you gotta get out—"

"Just stand still, Deputy," Adam Lee said from behind Bass Reeves. He had his gun pressed right into the small of the lawman's back.

Reeves ignored Lee and glared at Ben Jones with hurt and betrayal.

"Bass, I didn't—"

"I'll take this," Lee said, plucking Reeves's gun from his holster.

"And now what?" Reeves asked. "You gonna shoot me in the back?"

"Don't tempt me, Deputy," Lee said. "Ya'll know better den to tempt a desperate man."

"Bass . . ." Jones started, but he didn't know what to say.

"We jus' gon' wait for the rest of de boys," Adam Lee said, "and den you gon' help us rob the bank."

"I don't think so," Reeves said.

"Let's jus' back inta dis here alley and discuss it," Lee said, grabbing the back of Reeves's collar and pulling.

Clint saw two more black men ride into town and knew that he'd been right. Secretly, he'd been hoping not to disappoint Bass Reeves and steer him wrong. So he felt both satisfaction and concern about this. There were at least six bank robbers, and just him and Reeves to stop them.

He turned to look down at Reeves and his cousin and froze at what he saw. There were three black men down there. The first one who had ridden in was standing with his gun in Reeves's back.

"Damn it!" Clint said.

His first instinct was to run down there, but as they pulled Reeves into the alley he instinctively knew they weren't planning to kill him. It was more than likely they were going to use Bass to help rob the bank. And nothing was going to happen until the last of the men rode into town.

Clint considered running down to the end of town and stopping the next one or two black men who tried to ride in, but he could very well end up killing an innocent man that way, some poor slob who just happened to be riding into town.

He decided his best bet was to get himself as close to the bank as possible and wait. If ever his ability to hit whatever he pointed his gun at was going to come in handy, this was it.

FORTY-FOUR

As George rode into town with Otis, his head was spinning. Everybody's mind was on robbing the bank, but his mind was on Leona. He'd planned on killing Adam Lee because that would leave Leona free to be with him, and it would enable him to take over the gang . . . and then disband it. Tell everybody to go their own way. And then . . . and then what? He, Wanda, the children, and Leona would head south together? Neither woman would stand for that. And he couldn't see himself taking the children from Wanda. He'd never thought Leona was a good mother to her kids, why would he expect her to look after his? No, he needed Wanda to be a mother, and he needed Leona to be his whore.

But what if she was everybody else's whore, too? What if Ben had been telling the truth and she had been with him. Then how many others had there been?

Did he really think he was man enough to be all Leona needed?

"George," Otis said. His tone indicated it wasn't the first time he'd called George's name.

"What?"

"Whatchoo doin'? We got to ride over to the saloon."

"I don't see why we don't just ride up to the bank," George said.

"But Adam said—"

"Yeah, I know what Adam said. Come on."

George jerked the reins on his horse and directed him over to the bank.

"We're gonna need the horses here to get away," he told Otis.

"Adam got a plan—"

"I know he's got a plan," George said. "That don't mean I have to agree with it."

Otis looked over his shoulder, wondering when the last two men—Rafe and Lou—were going to come riding in.

George dismounted and Otis, unsure of what to do, followed.

George looked at Otis. Big, rangy, in his thirties. Had he been with Leona, too?

"Hey, Otis."

"Yeah?"

"What do you think of Leona?"

"What?"

"Leona, Adam's wife," George said. "You think she good-lookin'?"

"Man, that about the good-lookinist woman I ever did see," Otis said, "but don't tell my Rachel I said dat, I gets in lots of trouble. She hate dat woman!"

"Your Rachel is fine-lookin'," George said.

"I knows it, but dat Leona—hey, here come Rafe and Lou."

"Okay," George said. "We goin' in.

"We supposed ta wait for Adam and Ben."

"Ben's a young kid, he's gonna get us killed," George said. "The four of us can do it and we got our horses right here."

"But Rafe and Lou are gon' wanna wait—"

"We'll see," George said. "We'll see what they wanna do."

Rafe and Lou, he thought. *Two of the dumbest . . . was either of them with Leona?*

Rafe and Lou reined in their horses in front of the bank as they were supposed to.

"What you two doin' here?" Rafe hissed. "Dis ain't de plan."

"We got a new plan," George said.

"Who say so?" Lou asked.

"I say so," George said. "I'm takin' over."

"What for you takin' over?" Rafe demanded.

"Because of what Adam did to that fella at the trading post. That was crazy, and he's gettin' crazier by the minute."

"I guess dat's true," Otis said.

"Rafe? Lou? You with us? The four of us is takin' this here bank," George said.

Rafe and Lou exchanged a look, and then Lou said, "Let's get to it, then."

From across the street, near the hardware store, Clint watched the four black men dismount in front of the bank. It looked like it was time, but where were the other two men who'd been with Bass Reeves? If it was just these four men robbing the bank and if Clint got the jump on them as they came out, he might be able to stop them alone. He was going to have to trust in Bass Reeves's experience as a lawman to get himself out of trouble.

He loosened his gun in his holster, then picked up his rifle from where he'd had it leaning against the doorjamb. He was ready.

From down the street, peeking out of the alley, Ben Jones saw the four black men stop in front of the bank.

"Dey all in front of the bank," he said to Adam, who was deeper in the alley, still holding his gun on Bass Reeves.

"What?" Lee asked. "Dat ain't de plan. Dey supposed to wait for us to walk over dere—wit' dis here deputy, if we has him, which we do."

"Well, plan or no plan, dey goin' into the bank right now," Jones said.

"Son of a bitch!" Lee hissed. "Dey gon' ruin de whole thing."

"It was ruined the minute you grabbed me," Reeves said. "See, we got the bank covered."

"What?" Jones asked.

"I was tryin' ta warn you, kid," Reeves said. "I ain't been heard from in the last few minutes, so my men are surroundin' the bank."

"We can't go to the bank now!" Ben Jones told Lee.

"He lyin'," Lee said. "Ain't no way he coulda knowed we was comin' in today. He ain't got no men."

"He's right, Ben," Reeves admitted. "I'm lyin'. I don't have men. I have one man."

"Ha!" Adam Lee said. "One man ain't gon' be able ta stop no bank robbery."

"He will when it's the Gunsmith," Reeves said.

FORTY-FIVE

"There he is!" Ben Jones said.

"Who?"

"The Gunsmith," Jones said. "It got to be him. He standin' right in the middle of de street, waitin' for our boys ta come out."

"Dis is your fault," Lee said to Reeves, jabbing him in the belly with the barrel of his gun hard enough to drive the air from his lungs.

"Hey," Jones said, "you don't got to do that now. Let him go and we can go help the others."

"Are you crazy?" Lee asked. "Dat the Gunsmith out there, den I don't want no part o' him."

"B-but George, Otis, Rafe, and Lou don't know he be out dere waitin' on them."

"Well," Lee said, "dey gon' find out soon."

"But what we gon' do?"

"Me, I'm gon' kill this son of a bitch nigger and get outta here."

As Lee's hand tightened on the trigger to shoot the

bent-over deputy, Ben Jones said, "No," and humped him. The gun went off, but it was not pointed where it would do the most damage. The bullet went into Bass Reeves's side instead.

He grunted, grabbed his side, and slid away from the two grappling men. He wanted to help Ben, but he didn't know how bad he was hurt, so he slipped out of the alley.

Inside, Lee and Jones struggled with the gun and eventually it went off again. Jones felt a searing pain in his side and fell to the ground while Adam Lee just turned and ran toward the back of the alley.

Clint heard both shots, but couldn't afford to be drawn from the bank, especially if that's what the shots were for.

The door to the bank opened and the four black men came running out, carrying bank bags. They had heard the two shots and came out with their guns in their hands, but they still didn't expect to see some crazy white man in the street waiting for them.

"Get him!" George shouted.

Clint didn't hesitate. He started firing, picking the bank robbers off one at a time.

Otis fell to Clint's gun first, then Rafe. Lou almost got a shot off, but in the end his gun fell from his lifeless hand.

George had time to get on his horse while holding onto his bag of money. He wheeled the animal around and rode it into Clint. The impact spun him around and knocked him on his ass, but he held onto his gun. As he started to fire at the fleeing man, Bass Reeves suddenly staggered into the street and into the line of fire.

"Damn it!" Clint shouted. He got to his feet and ran to

Reeves, who had fallen to his knee, clutching his bloody side.

Ben Jones got to his feet, holding his side. He pulled his hand away and looked down at the blood on his palm.

"I'm shot," he said to himself. "Oh, Lord, I'm shot."

But he didn't feel shot. He still had strength in his legs and there wasn't much pain.

He heard the shots coming from the bank and ran out into the street. As he did so, he saw George riding toward him.

"George! George!" he yelled.

George saw him, veered his way, and barely slowed down as he grabbed the younger man's arm and pulled him up behind him.

"Where de others?" Jones shouted.

"Dead," George replied.

There was no time for any more conversation as the two men rode hell-bent for leather out of town.

"Bass?" Clint said, leaning over the fallen deputy.

"Ain't so bad," Reeves said, either to himself or to Clint. "Ain't so bad."

Clint looked at the fleeing black men on one horse, and decided there was nothing he could do about it. He looked up as he heard someone running toward him, saw several men, among them Sheriff Burton.

"I need a doctor," Clint said.

"I gotta get to the bank," Burton said.

"It's over down there. You got three dead bank robbers, but somebody better pick the moneybags off the street before they're gone. Meanwhile, you help me get him to a doctor."

"I still gotta—"

"If you don't help me take him to the doctor, I'll put a bullet in you myself!" Clint said coldly.

Burton holstered his gun and grabbed one of Bass Reeves's arms.

FORTY-SIX

The doctor came out of surgery, wiping his hands on a towel.

"How is he?" Clint asked.

"I got the bullet out," Doctor Thaddeus said. "It didn't hit anything vital. He's got some burns from the powder, but other than that he should be okay. You can go in if you want. I just want him to lie there for a little while, and then you better get him a hotel room and a bed for a few days."

"Thanks, Doc."

Clint entered the room, found Reeves lying on an examining table with a sheet up to his chest.

"How many did you get?" Reeves asked.

"Three," Clint said. "I saw two get away—the one from the bank and your cousin."

"So that makes three that got away," Reeves said, "including the one that shot me. Ben saved my life, Clint. Kept that third one from shootin' me in cold blood."

"He did a good thing, then," Clint said. "Maybe he deserves a break."

"I think he may've got shot, too, though," Reeves said. "You got to go after them."

"I am," Clint said. "I just wanted to make sure you were okay."

"I'm okay," Reeves said, "and I'd get on a horse if that sawbones would let me."

"Never mind," Clint said. "You'd bleed to death before we got out of town."

"Then you go," the black deputy said, "and you go now. Here." He held out his badge.

"Not again."

"Take it," Bass Reeves said. "It'll be like I'm with ya."

"Jesus," Clint said, taking the badge, "how can I say no now?"

"You get 'em," Reeves said. "They'll be leavin' a trail even you can follow now."

"I'm going to leave before all the compliments go to my head."

"Bring the boy back," Reeves said. "I don't care about the others, but bring the boy back alive."

"I'll do my best, Bass."

When Clint left the doctor's office, the sheriff was waiting outside.

"We recovered most of the moneybags," he said. "They got away with one—but it was the one with the most money in it, maybe fifteen thousand."

"That much?"

"Probably not that much in the other bags put together. They probably could've got it all into two bags, but the teller said they seemed to each want a bag."

"You putting together a posse?" Clint asked.

"Yeah, you gonna ride with us?"

"I'm going ahead," Clint said, "leaving now before the trail goes cold."

"Alone?"

"Unless you want to come with me."

"Naw," Burton said, "I got to stay here and assemble the posse."

"Right."

"You got no standing," Burton called out to him.

Clint turned and showed him the deputy's badge.

"That ain't legal," Burton said. "You ain't been sworn in by a judge."

"I got all the standing I need," Clint said, touching his gun, "right here."

"You kill anybody, I'll have to take you in."

"But you won't," Clint said, "because you'll be happy I got them before you got there."

George tightened the bandage around Ben Jones's waist, made from the boy's own shirt.

"It ain't bad," he said. "Just a crease. The bullet ain't even in there."

"I never been shot before, George," Jones said. "It didn't hurt when it happened, but it hurts like the devil now."

"What happened, Ben?" George asked. "What happened to Adam?"

"He tried to shoot Bass, and I stopped him," Jones said, "but then he shot me."

"Son of a bitch."

"It was an accident," Jones went on, "we was strugglin' for the gun, but after the shot he just . . . ran. I tried to get him to go to the bank to help you and the others, but he wouldn't."

"And now they're all dead, except for us, and Adam," George said.

"George, Adam said you didn't follow the plan."

"Yeah, well," George said. "I thought I had a better one. Turns out I was wrong. Come on, let's get you to your feet. They'll be comin' for us."

"We goin' back to camp?"

"No," George said, "that's where Adam will be goin', but we won't be there, and neither will anyone else."

"Why not?"

"Let's get mounted," George said, "and I'll explain it to you."

They'd only ridden a short way when George finished telling Ben Jones about his plan.

"So all de women and children have moved?" he asked.

"That's right."

"Why?"

"I was gonna kill Adam, Ben, just like you and everybody else wanted me to."

"Everybody?"

"Some of the others," he said. "And we been in that one place too long. I figured with the bank money we could move on."

"Well, at least we got one bag."

"Yeah," George said, and he knew his bag had been the fullest.

"But Adam's still out there, George," Jones said. "He gon' come lookin' for all of us."

"Yeah, he is, Ben," George said, "and we'll be ready for him."

FORTY-SEVEN

Clint rode out of town and started looking for tracks. Like Reeves said, they were there, so clear even he could follow them. He dismounted to take a closer look, hoping for something distinctive that would help him continue to identify it. He found what he wanted, a small chink in one part of the horseshoe. Not much, but it would help.

He mounted up and started tracking . . .

Adam Lee pushed his horse to the limit getting back to camp. He was disappointed that no one was there, because his anger was such that he'd been planning to kill somebody.

He looked in all the buildings and found everybody gone—including his own wife and children—with all the supplies they could carry.

Well, they wouldn't be hard to follow. They had the supplies and the kids in that old buckboard. That thing was going to be so heavy it would leave ruts in stone.

•   •   •

George didn't stop again until they reached the abandoned barn where he'd told Wanda and Leona to take the others. As he rode up to it they came outside, the two women standing side by side. He could tell they hadn't been getting along with each other just from the way they stood, with plenty of room between them.

He reined in and let Ben Jones slide down to the ground before dismounting.

"What happened?" Leona asked.

"Are you all right?" Wanda asked him.

"Yeah, but Ben, here, got shot. It ain't bad, but it should be cleaned."

"Come on, Ben," Wanda said. She had shown concern for George and an eagerness to help Ben. Leona had shown neither of these traits.

"What happened? Did you get the money?" she asked as Wanda look Jones into the barn.

Instead of answering, he grabbed her arm and lowered his voice.

"How many of the men in this group have you been with?" he demanded.

"W-what are you talkin' about?"

"Don't play games with me, Leona," he said. "Not anymore. Ben told me you and him have been together, and that you love each other."

"Ben? Why, he's just a boy."

"Is it true?"

"That we love each other? No, but—"

"The other part? You and him?"

"Oh, it happened one time," she said. "It was after we were together the second time. I was waiting for you in those trees again, but it was Ben who came along by accident."

"So you grabbed him and did it with him because I wasn't there?"

"Well . . . yeah," she said. "I was waitin' for you, and I was all hot and itchy down there." She touched his arm. "It didn't mean nothin', George. Not like with us."

"And you ain't been with any of the others? Otis? Rafe?"

"They're married men!"

"So am I, but we been together."

"That's different," she said. "We belong together. Is that the money? How much did we get?"

"Ain't you gonna ask me where the others are? Or where your husband is?"

"I figured you killed Adam," she said. "Wasn't that what you was gonna do?"

"Well, I didn't," George said. "He's out there somewhere, lookin' for us."

"And . . . the others?"

"Rafe, Lou, and Otis are all dead," George said. "Killed by the Gunsmith, who was workin' with Bass Reeves."

"So we got Adam, Bass Reeves, and the Gunsmith lookin' for us?" she asked. "Baby, we better get out of here."

"I got to tell the other women their men ain't comin' back," he said, "and then we can all go—"

"No, baby," she said, putting her hand on his arm, "I mean just you and me. We got to go, and take the money with us."

"We can't do that, Leona," he said. "We can't leave these people. I can't leave my children. Can you leave yours?"

"I sure can," she said. "I'm tired of bein' Adam Lee's wife and mother to his kids. Let him have them."

"He's crazy!"

"And that's why we got to get out of here," she said.

"We get on your horse and go. Along the way we buy me a horse, and then we light out, maybe for Mexico."

"And take all the money?"

"Most of it, anyway," she said. "Leave a little behind if you want."

"What about Ben?"

"Kill Ben," she said. "Adam's gonna kill him anyway, when he finds him."

"Leona, when did you get so bloodthirsty?"

"I ain't bloodthirsty, baby," she said, touching his crotch. "I'm thirsty for you and me to be together. Come on, don't you wanna put it in my mouth, have me suck you until you—"

"Stop it!" he said, swatting her hand away. "That's not gonna happen, ever again."

"You don't think so?" she asked, arching an eyebrow. "What if I tell Wanda what's been goin' on?"

"She won't believe you."

"She won't?" she asked. "You got yourself a real peculiar little scar down there, lover. What if I tell her I seen it?"

He had a scar on his inner thigh that only a woman who was with him could have seen.

"You say one word to Wanda, Leona," he said, "and I'll not only kill your husband, I'll kill you, too."

"You gon' make my kids orphans?"

"Me an' Wanda will take 'em and raise 'em with our kids," George said. "They won't miss you or their father at all. Think about it."

He went into the barn to see how Ben Jones was doing, leaving the moneybag on his horse.

FORTY-EIGHT

The going was slow for Clint, who had always left the tracking to the experts. Following a bunch of riders would have been easier than trying to track this one horse. He knew there were times he had to dismount to pick up the trail that Bass Reeves would have just kept on going. At sixty, Reeves still had eyes like a hawk. Clint felt like he had the eyes of an owl as he squinted again and again to pick up the trail.

It was simpler for Adam Lee. He just had to track the trail of the buckboard, which was easy. The longer it took, though, the madder he got. He hoped that somebody had gotten away from the bank with some money, because whoever it was, he was going to kill them and take the money from them. After that he'd ride off with it, leaving everybody—women, children, whoever—behind. It was time for Adam Lee to take care of himself.

Time for him to truly be a free man.

• • •

George watched as Wanda and one of the other women cleaned and bandaged Ben Jones's wound. They did it in silence, except for the crying of two of the other wives, who were grieving for their men. The woman helping Wanda was Otis's wife, who seemed to be holding up well after the news that her husband was dead.

"No good lazy nigger, anyway," she'd mumbled with wet eyes, but that had been the sum total of it for her.

The children were in another part of the barn, playing quietly, some of them unaware that their fathers were dead.

"Those poor babies," Wanda said. "How dey gonna take it?"

"I don't know," George said. "Is Ben gonna be able to ride?"

"I'll ride," Ben said.

"We got our two horses, and we'll get the rest of 'em on the buckboard—"

Suddenly, they all became aware of the sound of a horse. At first George thought it was an approaching horse, but then he realized it was a departing horse.

"Damn it!" he shouted and ran outside. Sure enough, Leona had taken his horse and ridden off with the money. He could still see the cloud of dust she had kicked up, but she was out of sight, having already topped a rise and gone from view. She was heading south, though. He guessed she was serious about going to Mexico.

He ran back into the barn.

"Ben, I got to take your horse."

Wanda stood up and grabbed his arm.

"Let her go, George," she said with sad eyes. "We don't need her . . . do we?"

George looked into his wife's eyes and realized that she

knew. His wife knew that he'd been with Leona, and suddenly, he felt ashamed.

"I gotta go, Wanda," he said. "She's got the money. Maybe we don't need her, but we need that money. Otherwise we got no place to go."

"All right," she said, taking her hand away. "You go and get the money. We'll wait here."

"Ben," George warned, "Adam might show up here. Or somebody from town."

"I'm ready."

"Even if it's Bass Reeves?" George asked.

"I be ready, George," Jones said.

George nodded, looked at Wanda, and said, "I'll be back before ya know it."

"You be careful of dat woman, George," Wanda said. "She be evil."

"I know, Wanda," George said. "I know."

FORTY-NINE

Adam Lee stared down at the abandoned barn. The buck-board tracks led right into it. There was no movement, but he didn't want to ride into a trap. He didn't know who had gotten away from Sherman, or if they'd even made it with money. He knew he'd shot Ben Jones, but he didn't know how bad. He decided to dismount and go down to the barn on foot, leading the horse behind him.

He got right up to the building and still nobody was showing. He did hear voices, though, the voices of children. He dropped his horse's reins to the ground, moved up to the front door slowly. He peered around, saw the women and children, and only one man: Ben Jones, who was sitting on the ground with a bandage around his waist. There were no horses. Either nobody had made it out of town, or they just weren't there yet.

He stepped into the barn with his rifle leveled at Ben Jones.

It was Wanda, George's wife, who saw him. She said, "Put that rifle down, Adam Lee."

"Adam!" Jones said, and went for his gun. Lee shot him dead center.

"Ain't gon' need no bandage this time."

"You killed him!" Wanda screamed. "He was just a boy."

"He was a boy full growed, Wanda," Lee said. "Full grown enough to have carnal relations with my wife—just like your husband did."

Wanda raised her chin.

"Your wife is an evil woman, Adam Lee," she said. "She cast a spell on dem men."

"Maybe," Lee said, "but they both gon' die for it. Where is George?"

"He ain't here," she said, "and neither is Leona. What dat tell you?"

"Is dere any money?" he asked.

Before Wanda could say anything, one of the other wives said, "Your wife ran off wit' de money, and George is chasin' her. Now leave us an' our babies be."

Wanda silently cursed the woman for her big mouth. She had wanted to make Lee believe that George and Leona had run off together, and then misdirect him as to which way they went.

"Which way did they go?" he asked.

"North," Wanda said immediately.

"Dat's a lie," Lee said.

"Dey went south," the same woman said.

"Dat's a lie, too. I come from the south."

"Dey went southwest."

He thought about it. That's where he would go if he had Leona and a lot of money—to Mexico.

Lee walked over to Jones and kicked him to make sure he was dead.

"Don't be kickin' de dead!" Wanda shouted.

"You shut yer mouth, woman," he said. "You can't even satisfy your own man, he got to go sniffin' around my woman."

"Well, if you was satisfyin' your woman she wouldn't hafta go sniffin' around my man."

For a moment it looked as if Wanda had gone too far and Lee was going to kill her.

"You shoot her you gon' hafta shoot me, too," said the woman who had told him about George and Leona.

"Me, too," one of the other women said, standing in front of Wanda.

"And in front of your own babies," the last woman said.

Lee looked over at his kids, who were watching him with wide eyes.

"You can all go to hell." He turned, stalked out of the barn, mounted his horse, and headed southwest.

The women ran to young Ben Jones's side, but he was as dead as could be.

Clint finally tracked the horse to what looked like an abandoned barn. He rode down most of the way to it, then went the rest of the way on foot, leading Eclipse. When he got down there, he could hear the voices of women and children. When he looked into the barn, that was all he saw. He walked right in with Eclipse behind him.

"Whatchoo want?" a woman demanded.

"I'm sorry, ma'am," he said, "but I guess I'm looking for your husbands."

The woman—Wanda—placed her fists on her ample hips and asked, "Who you be?"

"My name's Clint Adams, ma'am."

One of the women ran for Ben Jones's handgun, which

was lying on the ground next to his blanket-wrapped body. Clint saw what she was doing, got there just as she picked it up. He grabbed her wrist and took the gun away from her.

"Now why would you want to do that?" he asked.

"'Cause your de man killed her husband," Wanda said, "and their husbands."

"I'm sorry if I did that, ma'am," he said, "but they were robbing a bank."

"Whatchoo want here?"

"There were some men who got away," he said. "I suspect this poor fellow was one of them. Who is it?"

"His name's Ben Jones," one of the women said.

"Bass Reeves's cousin," Clint said.

"Yes."

"So who does that leave?"

"My husband, George Washington," Wanda said, finally deciding to just tell the truth. "He after Leona, who took the moneybag and run. And den her husband, Adam Lee. He after both of dem."

"George Washington?" Clint asked.

"It a fine name!" Wanda said, proudly.

"Yes, ma'am, it is," he said. "Uh, if you'll kindly tell me which way they went, I might be able to keep anybody else from gettin' killed."

"Dey went southwest, headin' for ol' Mexico," Wanda said, "and you do us all a favor if you make sure dat devil woman end up dead."

"Ma'am," he said, "I don't think that's something I can promise."

FIFTY

Leona didn't know where she was going, or what she was doing. All she knew was that she had the money and she had left behind her the life that was killing her, strangling her. Even though she didn't know what lay ahead of her—literally—she wasn't going back, ever.

George knew he was closing in on Leona. She was not a good rider, and she didn't really know where she was going. He figured she stole the horse and money on impulse. Of course, if she happened to run into a man alone she'd get him to help her. Poor fella. Nobody could resist Leona—but Leona and money?

He wished he knew how much was in that bag.

Adam Lee was no tracker, but he could smell Leona and George ahead of him. They were probably together now, because once George caught up to her, he wouldn't be able to resist her.

It was odd how the only man able to resist the woman was her husband.

Clint was finished tracking. Now he was just riding hard, pushing Eclipse, hoping to catch up to all the parties concerned before they killed each other. Actually, it wouldn't be bad if they killed each other, because then he'd be able to just pick up the bag of money and bring it back.

He thought about the women and children in the barn with the dead man. They were more alone now than they had been when their men got laid off from the ranches. There were only two husbands still alive, so what would they do now? Share one if he survived? And if both were killed? What then?

Clint figured he was going to have to take them all in to Sherman and let Bass Reeves sort it out. After all, it was his job, and they were his people. Clint reasoned that once he recovered this bank money, he was out of it for good.

Served him right for getting involved in the first place.

George could see the dust cloud being kicked up by Leona's horse. He was closing the gap, and he still hadn't decided what he would do when he caught her. He wanted the money back, and they would need the horse, but what should he do with her? What should he do, leave her stranded? Again, she'd only need to come across one man and she'd get him to help her. But what if the man who found her was her husband? Would Lee kill her? And how could a woman leave her own children behind?

Leona could hear the horse behind her. Somebody was chasing her. She didn't know if it was George, or Adam.

Probably George. Adam might not have even found that barn yet.

She looked ahead at the land spread out ahead of her. *Which way to go?* she wondered. *Which way to Mexico?*

And that was when her horse stumbled and went down, pitching her over the animal's head . . .

George saw Leona's horse go down, saw her go flying, had seen that happen to cowboys who landed and broke their necks. His mouth went dry, his heart started beating faster. He didn't know why. Was he hoping she was dead, or alive?

It had been hours since the bank robbery and the sun was going down. If Clint didn't catch up to somebody pretty soon, he'd be stumbling around out here in the dark. He doubted that the woman they were chasing—if she had the money, ultimately, it was she he was chasing—knew enough about the country to travel in the dark.

Out here the dark could kill the inexperienced.

Leona lay on her back and tried to catch her breath. She wondered if she was hurt bad. She had seen cowboys thrown this way by their horses end up with broken necks or backs. She tried to get her breath, wondered where the horse was. Had it gotten up and run off with the money tied to the saddle? Wouldn't that just be her luck? Or was it lying somewhere nearby with a broken leg.

Was that her horse she heard, or someone else's?

Suddenly, she was able to take a deep breath, and her arms and legs worked.

George rode to where Leona was lying, wondering if she was dead. The horse—his horse—had gotten back to its feet and was standing off to the side, favoring one leg. He couldn't tell if it was broken or not, but his first concern was Leona.

He dismounted and rushed over to her as her arms and legs began to move. The fall had hiked her dress up to her waist, revealing her to be naked beneath it. He couldn't help himself, found that he was looking at her thighs and at her pubic patch. In spite of himself, and the situation, he felt himself getting hard while he was looking at her. He felt lust and shame at the same time. Would it have been better if she were dead, killed by the fall? Or would his body be reacting the same way to hers, even if she'd been dead?

Now he just felt embarrassed.

FIFTY-ONE

George leaned down over Leona and pulled her dress down before even speaking to her.

"Are you all right?"

"I . . . just need . . . to catch . . . my breath . . ."

"Move your arms and legs?" George said. "I want to see if anythin's broke."

She did as he asked while continuing to catch her breath.

"Now move your head."

"I'm . . . all right . . . George," she said. "Nothin's broke. Help me sit up."

"Are you sure—"

"Come on, George!"

He helped her to a seated position and her breath began to come more easily.

"You're lucky you didn't break your neck," he said.

"It wouldn't've happened if you wasn't chasin' me," she said.

"So this is my fault?"

"It's all your fault, George," she said. "If you had killed Adam when we first talked about it—"

"You talked about it, not me," he said. "I'm gonna go check your—my—horse."

He walked over to the animal and checked both front legs. There was a gouge on the left one, but it didn't look too bad. The horse had been incredibly lucky, just like Leona. Usually a fall like that would have broken a leg on one of them.

He grabbed the moneybag from the saddle and checked to make sure it was still full of cash.

"Do you think I had time to get rid of the money and replace it?" she demanded from the ground.

"I'm just checkin', Leona," he said. "To tell you the truth I wouldn't put nothin' past you."

"Good," she said, "because there's nothin' I wouldn't do, George, to get away."

"Away from what? Your family? Your children?"

"All of it," she said, rubbing her hands together to get rid of the dirt. "I want out, George. Just give me a little money and let me go, take the rest back. Just gimme a few hundred, a thousand. Somethin' to get me started somewhere else."

"You don't need money to get started somewhere else, Leona," he said. "All you need is a man."

"I had me a man and look where it got me," she said. "Then I thought I had another man who was gonna help me get away."

"Me?" he asked. "You thought I was gonna leave my kids for you?"

She laughed at him and said, "I know you would've, George. I just needed a little more time, is all."

•   •   •

Adam Lee saw them together down there, Leona on the ground where she probably had fallen. He also saw that George was holding a moneybag from the bank.

He could have killed them both from here, but he heard the sound of a horse behind him. Quickly, he took cover behind some trees and watched the white man ride by. It had to be Clint Adams, and there was only one way he could ever hope to kill the Gunsmith.

From ambush.

He was just going to have to wait before he got all of them and took the money.

Clint saw the black man and black woman talking. She was on the ground. He was standing over her, holding the moneybag. Clint dismounted and decided to walk Eclipse the rest of the way. They were so involved with each other they'd never see him coming.

"Come on, George," she said. "One hundred. I'll have sex with you right here for a hundred dollars." She pulled her dress all the way up so he could see her crotch, belly, and breasts.

"Cover yourself up now, Leona," he said. "You a whore now?"

She yanked the dress down and said, "A woman's a whore from the minute she gets married, George. Don't you know that?"

"That's an interesting take on marriage."

They both turned their heads to see who had spoken. When George saw Clint, he recognized him from the front of the bank. His eyes went to his rifle on his saddle.

"Don't even think about it. You'd never make it."

"Who's this, George?" Leona demanded. "A new partner?"

"That's it, miss," Clint said. "I'm your new partner, only I'm taking the money back to the bank."

"This here's Clint Adams," George said. "He was workin' with Bass Reeves. He killed Rafe, Lou, and Otis at the bank."

"They didn't give me much of a choice," Clint said, "but I'm giving you one . . . George, is it?"

"That's right."

"Toss the moneybag over here, George."

It was the size of a carpetbag, had a handle, and was held closed by a strap and buckle. George looked down at it, enjoying the weight of it. He still didn't know how much was in it, but it felt good.

"Come on, do it, George."

"Mister," she said, "why don't you just kill him and you can have the money and me?"

"As tempting as that is, ma'am, I don't think I can do that."

"Don't call me ma'am," she said, annoyed. "I ain't no old lady."

"No, m-miss, I can see that. George, toss the bag at my feet . . . easy."

George swung the bag back and forth a couple of times, then let it go. It landed right at Clint's feet.

"How bad is that horse hurt?" Clint asked.

"Not too bad."

"I'll have to look at it, but first we need to make camp for the night."

"Why don't we just go back?" George asked.

"It'll be dark soon. I don't know how bad that horse is, and to tell you the truth, I'm kind of tired from chasing the two of you. So we're going to make a fire, then I'm going to tie the two of you up and check the horse."

"He's gonna tie us up and take the money for himself, George," Leona complained.

"I don't think so, Leona," George said. "Ain't everybody as bad as you think."

"Thank you, George," Clint said. "I appreciate the compliment. Now help the lady up and we'll all go look for some wood for a fire."

"You expect me to build a fire?" Leona asked.

"Miss, you're going to help build a fire, and unsaddle the horses—or I can just tie you up now while George and I do it."

She glared at him.

"George," Clint said, "why don't you help the lady to her feet and we can get started?"

"Mister," Leona said as George yanked her up, "this ain't no way to treat a lady."

FIFTY-TWO

When the horses were cared for and the fire going, Clint tied and secured George and Leona, then got some beef jerky from his saddlebags.

"You want some?" he asked them.

"I do," George said, "but I can't eat it with my hands tied behind me."

"We can fix that."

Clint moved around the fire, got behind George, and untied him. He handed him a piece of jerky, then moved over to Leona. He knew Leona for what she was, the kind of woman sex just oozed out of. Even as sweaty and dirty as she was, the smell of her reached right down inside and gave him a tug. Being this close to her made him hard.

"You want some?"

"You ever been with a black woman before, Mr. Gunsmith?" she asked, licking her full lips.

"As a matter of fact, I have," Clint said. "Just recently. And I found the experience very pleasant."

"But you ain't never been with a black woman like me," she pointed out.

"Miss," Clint said, "I don't think I've ever been with a woman like you, period—black or white. Now, do you want something to eat?"

She turned her head away from him and didn't answer.

"Leona, she ain't used to not gettin' her way with a man," George told Clint.

"I can believe it," Clint said, moving back around to the other side of the fire. "George, if you try anything while you're untied I'm going to have to shoot you."

"I understand."

"What happened to Leona's husband?" Clint asked. "He was at the barn before me. He never caught up to you?"

"Adam found the barn?" George asked.

"What'd he do?" Leona asked.

"He killed Ben," Clint said.

"Jesus . . ." George said.

Leona swore, but it wasn't because Ben had been killed. It was because another one of her conquests had let her down.

"He was ahead of me," Clint said again. "He should have caught up, unless . . ."

"Unless what?"

"Unless he heard me coming," Clint said, "and he's out there in the dark."

"He's waitin' till you fall asleep, then he's gonna kill you both and set me free. Me and Adam, we'll run off with the money."

"You'll both run out on your own children?" Clint asked.

"They'll be better off with Wanda, or one of the other women," Leona said. "If George is still alive, him and Wanda can raise them."

"You think Adam would take you with him?" George asked. "After what you've done?"

"He don't know what I done," she said. "I'll tell him you made me run off with you and the money. He'll believe me."

"Leona," George said, "I do believe Adam is the only man you can't wrap around your little finger—well, him and Mr. Adams, here."

"Call me Clint," Clint said. "Since I may have to kill you, we might as well be on a first-name basis."

"Clint, what you think a man gon' do to a woman who cheat on him with other men, and run out on their kids and steal money from him?"

"All that?" Clint asked. "I guess he'd do just about anything, maybe even kill her."

"He ain't gonna kill me, he loves me."

"All men love you, Leona," George said, "and we all wanna kill you."

"I can understand that."

"What you understand?" Leona asked. "You wanna understand, you untie me and have me right here by the fire, then maybe you understand."

"As tempting as that is, Leona," Clint said, "I think I'll just keep you tied up."

"Well, then, I'm hungry."

"Now you're hungry? I asked you—"

"I wasn't then."

"Well, you wait until George finishes, then when I tie him back up, I'll untie you and give you some jerky."

"How much money is in that bag, Clint?" George asked, indicating the bag next to Clint's feet.

"You don't know?"

George shook his head.

"Never had a chance to count it. I know it was the heaviest bag."

"They tell me this bag has more money in it than all the others combined."

"How much?" Leona asked, her eyes glittering in the firelight.

"If I tell you," Clint said, "either of you, I think you'd do just about anything to get it from me."

"That much, huh?" George asked.

FIFTY-THREE

Adam Lee sat out in the dark with no campfire and no food. He stared down at the three figures sitting around the fire. He was not a good enough marksman to kill the Gunsmith from here. He would have to get closer, and he would do that just before first light, when he could see, but would still have some cover.

Since the Gunsmith had Leona and George tied up, it was only the gunman Lee was going to have to worry about. Once he was gone, the other two would be at his mercy—a thought that delighted him.

He wanted the money, and he wanted his revenge.

At first light Clint rolled out of his blanket and checked his captives. Sometime during the night they had huddled together in their sleep. He had a feeling those two had been huddled together before.

Clint put the fire out, then lifted his head when Eclipse nickered at something. He stood up and looked around in all directions. If Adam Lee was out there, he might be angling for a clear shot, but Clint doubted the man was a marksman. He'd have to get close, and maybe that was what Eclipse had sensed. There was some high grass around, and Lee could have been lying flat in it. There wasn't much in the way of cover, except off in the distance where there were some trees.

Clint walked to Eclipse and patted the horse's massive neck.

"Good boy," he said. "You probably scared him away."

Which was exactly what happened, although Lee didn't know anything about the horse alerting Clint. He just thought the man had instincts that had somehow given him away.

He started forward, using the high grass, but suddenly Clint Adams had stood up and started looking around. Lee froze, and when Clint walked over to the horse, Lee backed away to safety.

He was going to have to wait for another opportunity. He could follow them when they left, but the Gunsmith's instincts would probably give him away then, too.

Then he realized what his next move should be, and felt calmed by the decision. Everything was going to work out, after all.

"Wake up."

Clint kicked George just hard enough to wake him. The man woke with his face pressed to Leona's left breast. He reared back, as if the breast had burned him. Leona, un-aware, woke and rubbed her eyes.

"I'm hungry," she said.

"So am I," Clint said. "You'll have to wait until we get back to the rest of the women."

Oddly, that was all that was left of the black cowboy gang—their women.

"You think those bitches gonna share their food with me?" she asked, laughing. "In fact, ya'll might as well shoot me now, 'cause they gonna kill me when we get back."

"Why? What did you do to them?"

"Their husbands all wanted me," she said. "Ain't that enough reason for them to hate me?"

"I suppose," Clint said, "if I looked at it from a woman's point of view."

He checked their bindings and got them to their feet.

"You ain't gonna make us travel tied up?" she asked.

"Oh, but I am."

Clint had saddled all the horses. The night before he'd checked the injured horse, and managed to bandage the leg using an old shirt in his saddlebag. If they didn't push it, he thought the animal would make it back.

"Let's get you up on your horse," Clint said to Leona.

"That's my horse," George said. "She stole it. I'll ride it."

"Fine," Clint said. He grabbed Leona, lifted her into his arms, and walked to the other horse. He was very aware of the heat of her body. She put her head on his shoulder and let her lips just brush his neck. Annoyingly, he was hard again.

He flung her up onto the saddle abruptly, so that she came down hard.

"Ow!"

"Serves you right," he said. "Behave."

He turned and saw George grabbing the saddle horn with his bound hands and hoisting himself into the saddle. Clint walked over to Eclipse and mounted up.

"You think Adam gonna try to kill us and take the money?" George asked.

"You know him better than I do," Clint said. "What do you think?"

"He's gone crazy," George said, "so I say hell, yeah. I just don't know how he expect to take it away from you."

"I guess we'll just have to find out," Clint said.

FIFTY-FOUR

Clint didn't like it.

As far as he could tell, there was no one following them. Was Adam Lee the kind of man to give up? After all, he ran out on all his partners in Sherman when things went bad. But according to George, the man had lost his mind, so there was no telling what he would do.

"He ain't back there, is he?" George asked.

"How do you know?"

"You keep lookin' back and you don't look happy."

"No, he's not following us, unless he's really good at it."

"He ain't," Leona said. "He ain't really good at much of anythin'."

"Would he give up?" Clint asked.

"Oh, no," she said, "ain't no give up in him, neither. He'll just keep goin' until he messes everythin' up. That's his style."

"Why was he the leader of your group, then?" Clint asked George.

"He wanted to be," George said. "Nobody else did."

"Not you? You sound pretty smart to me."

Leona "*hmph'd*" at that.

"I never wanted to be nobody's leader," George said. "I jus' wanna live my life. Everybody pushin' me, though, to take over."

"And did you try?"

"I made the wrong decision at the wrong time, when we got to the bank," George said. "It's my fault it all went wrong."

"Not really," Clint said. "We were waiting for you."

"How'd you know we were comin'?" George asked.

Clint shrugged.

"It was time for you to try a bigger job," Clint said. "We assumed the bank would be your best bet."

"You and Bass Reeves?"

"That's right."

"Now, he's a smart one," George said. "More of us should be like him."

Clint didn't bother telling George the bank was his idea.

"He's a smart one, all right."

"Ain't none of you smart," Leona said.

"None of who?" Clint asked.

"Men," she said. "White, black, don't make no never mind."

"You don't have much of an opinion of men, do you?" he asked.

"No," she said, "I ain't never seen the man who could give me a good opinion."

"Well," Clint said, "I'm afraid today's not going to be any different for you, Leona."

They came within sight of the barn and then Clint stopped.

"What's wrong?" Leona asked. "Come on. I'm hungry. I ain't eaten since yesterday."

"Shut up, Leona," George said. "You thinkin' Adam's down there?"

"That's what I'm thinking," Clint said.

"We ride down there and he start shootin'?"

"Maybe," Clint said. "How good is he with a rifle?"

"I tol' ya," Leona said. "He ain't good at nothin'."

"We'd hafta be closer for him to try it," George said. "I think maybe he'll wait until we get off our horses."

"And he's got a barn full of hostages," Clint said. "All women and children. Would he hurt them?"

"Yeah," George and Leona said at the same time.

"His own children are in there," Clint said.

"He do them last if he have to," Leona said, "but he do them."

"Well, I guess he is crazy, then," Clint said. "I'm going to have to handle him that way."

"You want me to go down?" George asked.

"He'd kill you as soon as he saw you," Clint said.

"Maybe when he kills me, you can kill him."

"Why would you do that?"

George shrugged.

"Ta make things right, maybe. Besides, my wife and kids is down there."

"Hmph," Leona said, "your wife."

"She's a good woman," George said, "not like you."

"Give me a few minutes to figure something out, George," Clint said. "If I let you ride down there, you're not going to light out on me, are you?"

"If I try, you a good enough shot to kill me before I gets too far."

"You're right about that."

"Then why would I do it?"

"You gon' believe him?" Leona asked. "He lyin', like every man lie."

"Shut up, Leona," George and Clint said at the same time.

FIFTY-FIVE

Adam Lee said to his son, Lucas, "Go to the door, boy, and see if anybody's out dere."

"Yes, Papa."

"Adam Lee, don't be sendin' dat baby—" Wanda started, but Lee turned to her and shouted, "Shut up, Wanda. Don't make me shoot you. Den who gon' watch your babies?"

The four-year old walked to the door, looked out, and returned.

"Well?"

"Dere's two men and a lady, Papa."

"Do you know the lady?"

"Yes, Papa. It's Momma."

"And is the man Uncle George?"

"I dink so."

"And who else."

"A white man."

"Okay," Lee said, "go sit with your sister."

The boy walked over to where his three-year-old sister

was sitting and plopped down next to her. The rest of the women and children were huddled against the same wall. Wanda reached out to gather in Lee's children and hold them with her own.

Lee walked to the door, pressed his back to it, held his rifle ready.

"I know you out dere," he shouted. "I got women and kids in here. I gon' start shootin' dem and t'rowin' de bodies out!"

A couple of the women caught their breath.

"You hears me out dere?"

"We hear you, Adam," George shouted. "I gon' come in."

"You ain't comin' in here, George Washintgon," Lee called. "You wanna send somebody in, you send Leona. You send my lovin' wife."

Clint had untied both George and Leona. If Leona wanted to run, that was her business. George, too, for that matter, although he didn't think the man would. But he took the moneybag with him when he circled around to the back of the barn, just to be on the safe side.

"This is crazy, George," Leona said. "Let's jus' get on these horses and go."

"No," George said, "we gon' do the right thing, Leona. For once. We gon' get all those babies out of there."

"I ain't goin' in there," she said.

"He'll start killin' kids," George said. "Your kids are in there, Leona."

"I don't care, I ain't goin' in," she said. "He'll kill me."

George turned to face her, towering over her.

"I'll kill you if you don't."

She gave him an arrogant grin.

"You ain't got a gun."

"I'll break your neck."

She stared up at him, her arrogance starting to fade away. "You ain't got the guts."

He glared at her and said, "Try me."

She stared up at him boldly and then, slowly, as if in stages, her face began to fall until she had to avert her eyes.

"You'd do it," she said in a whisper.

"I got nothin' ta lose, Leona," he said, "and my babies to save."

"You sendin' Leona in, George?" Adam Lee called out impatiently.

"I'm sendin' her now!" George called back, then lowered his voice and added to her, "Ain't I?"

"I'm comin' in, Adam," Leona shouted. She glared at George and added, "He do me a big favor if he shoots me dead."

Clint heard the voices from behind the barn. For an abandoned structure the back was remarkably well-preserved. There was a back door but it was barred from the inside. He used a space between some slats to look inside, saw a bunch of women and children up against one wall. They were too far away for him to catch someone's attention and get them to open the door.

He put the moneybag down on the ground and moved around to the other side of the barn. Maybe he could sneak all the way around and catch George when he stuck his head out. But as he moved around, he could hear that George was sending Leona in. It surprised him that Leona would go. He wondered if her husband would talk to her, or just go ahead and kill her?

It didn't matter really. He was too far out of position to do anything about it now.

FIFTY-SIX

As Leona reached the entrance to the barn, Lee grabbed his wife and yanked her in. Once inside, he backhanded her across the face.

"Whore!" he said. "Where's my money?"

She didn't even give him the satisfaction of touching her cheek, just glared back at him boldly.

"I don't have your money," she said.

"Who does?"

"A man you'll never get it from."

"The Gunsmith? Him?" he asked. "He's just a white man with a gun."

"Too much man for you."

"We'll see 'bout that. Who else is out there besides George?"

"Nobody?"

"Bass Reeves ain't about?"

"He's in Sherman. He got shot when you robbed the bank."

"Too bad."

"What else you wanna know, Adam?" she asked.

"Nothin'," Lee said. "I don't wanna know nothin' from you, bitch. I jus' want my money."

"You'll have to get it from the Gunsmith," she said, taunting him.

"No," Lee said, "I think I'll have the Gunsmith bring it to me."

"Clint Adams!"

Clint was moving along the far wall of the barn, almost to the front where he'd be able to get a look at the front entrance.

"Adams! I know you're out there," Lee called out. "You've got my money."

"It's not your money, Lee," Clint called back. "It belongs in the bank in Sherman."

"Well, a lot of people've died for that money," Lee said, "and I'm gon' have it. You bring it to me."

"Not a chance."

"I've got my gun on one of dese here kids," Lee said. "You don't bring me my money, I'll start killin' 'em. And I want you to toss out your gun."

Damn it, Clint thought.

"I want you and George out where I can see you."

Clint cursed himself for not grabbing his Colt New Line and sticking it in his belt. Once he gave up his gun, there was no telling what would happen.

Well, yes there was. He'd be dead.

"Adams! I ain't kiddin'," Lee shouted. "I'll kill dese here kids."

"Even your own?" Clint yelled.

"I want my money! Bring it to me!"

"Okay," Clint called out. "Okay. Give me a minute. I have to get it."

Clint headed for the back of the barn, where he'd left the moneybag.

Then Lee shouted to George, "Come closer, where I can see you."

George heard the conversation between Clint and Adam Lee, then heard Lee call for him.

"I'm comin'," George shouted back.

As he got closer to the barn, Lee called out, "Throw away your rifle."

George assumed that Lee could somehow see him, so he flung the gun away.

"Keep comin'."

Unarmed, George continued to the barn.

Clint got around behind the barn where he had left the moneybag and bent over to pick it up. He was startled to see a small face staring out at him from inside the barn. He could see the little face in between some of the wooden slats.

"Hey," he said.

"Hello."

"What's your name?"

"Lucas."

"Lucas, I'm Clint. Are you scared?"

"No."

"Lucas, can you unlock this back door for me?"

"Yeth."

"Okay," Clint said, "do it as quietly as you can. It's a surprise."

"I like surprises."

"I do, too."

Lucas didn't move.

"Lucas?"

"Yeth."

"Could you unlock it now?"

"Yeth."

The boy finally moved.

FIFTY-SEVEN

Adam Lee saw George come into view, was tempted to just shoot him down, but he decided to wait until he had Clint Adams in sight, as well.

"You recognize this little fella?" Lee asked George.

George saw that the little boy Lee had in front of him was his son, Emmett, who was the same age as Lee's son, Lucas.

"Adam," George said, "let the boy go. You got me now."

"Where's Adams?" Lee shouted. "I want my money."

"It's comin'," George said. "Stay calm, Adam."

"I be calm when I got my money!" Lee shouted.

George's heart was in his throat as he stared around, looking for some sign of Clint Adams. He couldn't just stand there and let his son die! If Clint didn't show up in the next five seconds, he was going to have to do something—anything, even if it meant taking a bullet.

Lucas was having trouble removing whatever was holding the door closed, but Clint kept talking to him in encouraging whispers, hoping no one else would hear and call attention to them. He knew he was taking a chance, putting everyone's life into the hands of this small child, but it was his only hope. Once Clint was disarmed, he was dead.

Finally, he heard something drop and the door was open!

"Good boy!" he said.

"That's it!" Lee said. "Too long. Say g'bye to your son, George."

"No!" George shouted. He started running straight at Adam Lee.

There was a shot.

"Hold it, Lee!" Clint shouted, stepping through the open back door.

Lee either didn't hear him, or was ignoring him, but Clint saw he had his rifle trained on the boy and heard him shout, "Say g'bye . . ."

"Lee!" Clint shouted again. He didn't want to back-shoot the man but he had no choice. He fired once.

Adam Lee felt the searing pain in his back. He released the boy, tried to bring his rifle to bear on George, but he only got it halfway up when all the strength seemed to drain out of him.

One shot, he just wanted to get off one shot . . .

Wanda rushed forward and grabbed her son, shielding him with her body. She heard the one shot and tensed . . .

George Washington saw Adam Lee stagger and fall, saw Wanda protecting their son. At least she was there for him . . .

•   •   •

Clint rushed to the fallen man and kicked his rifle away. He looked up as George reached the door.

"You okay?" Clint asked.

"Yeah."

They both looked at Wanda, who was holding Emmett.

"Your boy's okay, too."

"Thank you."

Clint nodded.

"I'm all right, too, if anyone cares," Leona said.

Clint looked at Leona. Her cheek was swollen from where her husband had hit her, and she was disheveled and dirty—and sexy as hell. *Another time,* he thought . . .

FIFTY-EIGHT

Clint and Bass Reeves entered the judge's chamber. The man behind the desk was a commanding presence. If he wasn't as arrogant as Judge Parker, they might get along.

"Mr. Adams," the judge said, "welcome. I understand we have a debt of gratitude to pay you."

"I don't know who *we* is, Judge," Clint said. "I was doing a favor for my friend Bass."

"Indeed." The judge looked at Reeves. "Are you recovered from your wound, Deputy?"

"Recoverin', sir," Reeves said.

"Good, good," the judge said. "And what about the families? The women and children?"

"We're tryin' ta place them somewhere, Judge," Reeves said. "With their husbands dead or in prison, we're tryin' to find some other family."

"And you, Deputy," the judge said. "You lost a family member."

"Yes, my cousin."

"You have my sympathy."

"Thank you, sir."

"The bank is happy that they've gotten their money back," the judge told them.

"That's good."

"Curiously," the judge said, "they were missing about two thousand of it. Any explanation for that? Either of you?"

"Not me," Clint said. "Bass?"

Here was the test. Clint didn't know if Reeves was going to be able to lie to the judge—he was such a stickler for the letter of the law.

"Judge, I can honestly say I didn't see where that money went."

Well, Clint thought, *not a lie but good enough.*

"Then I guess we're done here," the judge said, "unless I can convince you, Mr. Adams, to accept a badge."

"Not a chance, Judge."

"Hmm, very well. Thank you both."

Clint and Reeves got up and headed for the door.

"Deputy, if you'll come and see me in the morning I'll have an assignment for you," the judge said. "Meanwhile . . . take the rest of the day off."

"Thanks, Judge."

On the street in front of the building Clint said, "Thank you, sir? The rest of the day? You need a week off to heal."

"I'm fine."

"You want to get a beer before I leave town?" Clint asked.

"Sure."

They walked to the small saloon they'd drunk in last time, took two beers to a back table. It was early, and the place was empty.

"Thanks for lying to the judge about that money," Clint said.

"I didn't lie."

"Okay, but . . . it was kind of a lie of omission."

"I didn't see you give any money to the wives of the black cowboys. What was it? A hundred for each of them, and for each of their kids?"

"That's right."

"A hundred dollars is a lot of money to those people."

"They have no husbands to speak of," Clint said. "If they all stay together, they'll have about two thousand to work with. That is, unless you find some of their families—"

"I ain't lookin'," Reeves said. "I just said that."

"But Bass . . . that *was* a lie."

Reeves looked at Clint from over the rim of his beer mug and said, "So sue me."

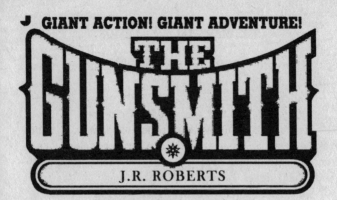

GIANT ACTION! GIANT ADVENTURE!

THE GUNSMITH

J.R. ROBERTS

Little Sureshot And
The Wild West Show
(Gunsmith Giant #9)

Dead Weight
(Gunsmith Giant #10)

Red Mountain
(Gunsmith Giant #11)

The Knights of Misery
(Gunsmith Giant #12)

The Marshal from Paris
(Gunsmith Giant #13)

penguin.com